To. DEREK,

CODENAME
DREDGE

Hope you ENJOY the RoAD!

Tony May

2008

TONY MAY SPENT THE EARLY years of his working career as a fabricator/welder travelling the world working in the oil and gas construction industry on both onshore and offshore facilities.

Returning to college in the late 1970s, Tony graduated with a degree in welding engineering and once more entered the petroleum construction industry, managing steel fabrication shops in several countries including Sumatra, Indonesia, Thailand and Kuwait at the conclusion of the 1991 gulf war in support of the oilwell fire fighters.

Tony is currently working on his third novel.

Published in Australia by Temple House Pty Ltd, T/A Sid Harta Publishers ACN 092 197 192 Hartwell, Victoria

Telephone: 61 3 9560 9920,
Facsimile: 61 3 9545 1742
E-mail: author@sidharta.com.au

First published in Australia 2005
Copyright © Tony May, 2005
Cover design, typesetting:
Chameleon Print Design

The right of Tony May to be identified as the Author of the Work has been asserted in accordance with the Copyright, Designs and Patents Act 1988.

This book is a work of fiction. Any similarities to that of people living or dead are purely coincidental.

May, Tony
Codename Dredge
ISBN: 1-921030-50-X
pp171

DEDICATION

To those who know the true law
Sakda, Somwong, Surasak, Churinthip,
Alannah, Ray and Boo.

Top: diagram of a dredge, and bottom: a dredge in action.

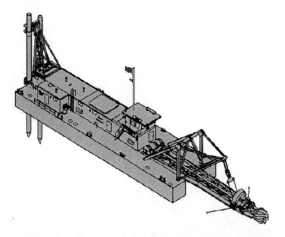

CHAPTER 1

Ａs I WAS EATING my first breakfast in the Landmark Hotel on Sukhumvit Road in the heart of Bangkok, the smiling waitress asked in her Thai-accented English, 'Would Farang like to read a Thai English newspaper?'

'Sure,' I told her, and as she handed me the latest edition of the *'Bangkok Post'*, I asked her what was the meaning of the word she had just called me. 'Farang', she explained, was the term Thai people call all white skin foreigners. I wasn't sure if I had been insulted or not.

The front-page headlines and following story aroused my curiosity.

"THE PLOT THICKENS

SAUDI ARABIAN JEWEL SCAM JUST GETS WORSE. POLICE GENERAL CHARGED WITH THE KIDNAPPING AND MURDERS OF THE WIFE AND TEENAGE SON OF A KEY PROSECUTION WITNESS.

According to reports, several off duty police officers stopped a Mercedes-Benz on a freeway in Bangkok, forced their way

into the vehicle, blindfolded and handcuffed the wife and son
and drove them away.

They were held hostage for several weeks. After their intern-
ment, they were both murdered, the killers placing their corpses
into the Mercedes. Late at night, the vehicle was parked across
an isolated highway in a manner so as to impede oncoming
traffic, a loaded semi-trailer truck slammed into the Mercedes.
Forensic specialists theorised murder but the Police General overruled the conclusion, labelling the deaths as traffic
fatalities. Authorities have since verified the original forensic
conclusion of murder.

An un-named Thai national, now serving a jail sentence,
was working in Saudi Arabia as a janitor in the palace of
King Faisal. He stole twenty million dollars worth of jewels
from the palace, smuggling them back into Thailand hidden
inside electrical appliances.

The precious stones were then fenced with three jewellers,
one of whom was the husband and father of the murdered
victims (who had been abducted in order to force him to release
information regarding the location of the stolen gems). The
now imprisoned Police General heading the investigation and
seven police officers on his task force were later charged with
malfeasance, conspiracy to embezzle and abuse of authority by
conspiring to kidnap and murder.

The Saudi Charge D'affaires' pressed the case for his Government, and Thailand's Prime Minister had his government
establish the 'Police Saudi Recovery Team', urging the public to
return the stolen items. Seventy percent of the precious stones were
returned to the Saudi's, however it was discovered later that some
of the returned jewels were fakes. In particular, a highly prized
blue pendant, wanted most by the Saudis, was never found.

During the period of the investigations, two Saudi diplomats
and a Saudi businessman were gunned down as they sat in

their vehicle waiting for traffic lights in the center of Bang-kok's business district. The two assassins, travelling on a black unmarked motorcycle, pulled up alongside the Mercedes-Benz carrying the Saudis, the passenger on the motorcycle opened fire, instantly killing all three. Due to dense traffic conditions, pursuit and capture at the scene was impossible."

As I put down the newspaper, I was thinking that was one hell of an article on crime, corruption and human greed, but Thailand sure didn't have the monopoly on that, news-papers worldwide are full of the same shit, only the players are different.

I had come to Thailand to work on an oil-refinery construc-tion project. The Bangkok company that hired me faxed the necessary entry documents, I forwarded them along with my passport to the local Thai Consulate in Calgary, Canada where I was then living. This procedure was required to obtain a non-immigrant visa, which would then be presented to the Thai immigration authorities on arrival, allowing me to obtain the appropriate work permit.

After several days of company orientation in the hugely populated, polluted and magical metropolis of Bangkok, I was transported to Pattaya City, Province of Chonburi, approximately one hundred and thirty kilometres south of Bangkok; this would be my place of residence for the next eighteen months.

Pattaya, with a population of approximately sixty–five thousand permanent residents plus thousands of foreign tour-ists and sex predators, sits on three major beaches—Wong Amat, Pattaya and Jomtien, all which help shape the shore-line of the Gulf of Thailand. The ocean waters sparkle under the daily brilliant sun that hangs in a mostly clear blue sky. It's easy living if you have a little cash, many individuals have parted with their money faster than anticipated, owing to the vast array of temptations—some intentionally, some not. A popular scam by many of the bar girls, organised by their local boyfriends, was to slip a chemical substance into the drink of some unsuspecting customer and when he woke up, both the girl and his cash were long gone.

Thailand is the center of a region that has become more and more frequented by visitors from many parts of the world. Its central location allows it to act as a gateway, with access roads, bridges, waterways and international airports to the surrounding countries of Burma, Laos, Cambodia and Malaysia, and with only short distances to Indonesia, China and Vietnam. The number of visitors to Thailand in 1998 reached roughly 7.7 million relating in tourism, being the largest foreign exchange earner, this revenue amounted to roughly 220 billion Baht. By comparison, revenue from the top export item, Thai Rice, was only 65 billion Baht, and the tourists just keep coming.

The refinery project was located in an industrial complex near the city of Maptaput, in the South-eastern Seaboard Province of Rayong, approximately sixty kilometres east of Pattaya City. I had been supplied with an Isuzu pick-up truck to transport myself to and from work.

At least three times a week, sometimes more, I would be pulled over by the local highway cops and told I had infringed some traffic law, which was mostly bullshit—all they wanted was cash. I would oblige with a hundred Baht bill (about four bucks US), they would thank me and tell me to be on my way. When I discussed this with other expatriates living in Pattaya, I was told of a common phrase that covered most everything strange in Thailand and that was 'TiT', meaning 'This is Thailand'. Well it wasn't worth worrying about those things I had no control over, so I didn't.

As the weeks rolled into months, I met several American Vietnam veterans who owned beer bars around Pattaya. They had come to Thailand after their war finished and stayed.

One of the bars was owned by a couple of Vets who had served in the original United States Navy Seal Team that had been engaged in battles along the Mekong River Delta. They told me that without the Vietnam War, Pattaya City would not have gained the sensual reputation, or the popularity it enjoys today. In the early sixties, American military personnel arrived at U-Tapao airport, approximately twenty-five kilometres east of Pattaya. The airport, at that time, was used as an airbase for B-52 bombers utilised over Vietnam. The military personnel, who had come to spend their R and R on the tranquil, palm-tree lined beaches of a quaint little fishing village, spread the word that Pattaya offered much by way of rest, and even more by way of recreation.

During my employment on the refinery project, I became friends with a Thai in his mid-fifties who had no problem with the English language. His position on the project was Safety Officer. Sakda had worked for many years in Saudi Arabia, telling me that since the jewellery scam, which I had read about my first morning in Bangkok, the Saudi's would not issue any more work permits to Thais until all the stolen items were returned. Sakda figured that meant never, as he believed that whatever jewels were still missing, would remain so. The longer I knew Sakda and the more Singha beer we drank, the more he told me of his past.

He had grown up on his father's farm near the city of Ubon, province of Ratchathani, which is located approximately ninety kilometres east of the mighty Mekong River, marking the border between Thailand and the Lao People's Democratic Republic.

When he was nineteen years old, a Thai-born Chinese

land-grabber swindled the family rice-paddy farm away from
his father. Sakda told me that early one morning as the swin-
dler was looking over his latest acquisition; he walked up
behind him with a loaded 22-calibre revolver and shot him
in the back of the head, killing him instantly, Sakda just
kept walking. As the eldest son, it was his duty to avenge
his father and his family, to 'save face' from the humility of
losing the farm.

Assassinations are a common occurrence to this day in
Thailand; sometimes the perpetrator is apprehended, sometimes not. After the killing, Sakda hired on with the United
States Air Force. The US ran an air base in Ubon, Ratchathani
for several fighter squadrons, which were utilised in the skies
over Vietnam.

After several indoctrination courses, the Air Force sent him
to Laos. Sakda had grown up speaking both the Thai and Lao
languages. His duties were to sit on a hilltop in the Plain of
Jars with US-supplied equipment and assist the B-52 bomber
aircraft crews with radio navigation as they came and went
on their bombing missions. He showed me several citations
the US Air force had awarded him for his participation and
endurance.

In the mid seventies, after the Vietnam conflict had ended,
people in Bangkok whom he knew to be local Mafia involved
in the sex-slave trade, hired Sakda. His assignment was to
fly to Japan acting as an escort for six to eight young Thai
girls, there they would be used as bar girls controlled by the
Japanese Mafia. His cover was a salesman for kid's toys. His
obligation was to take care of the visa documentation as he
and the girls, most of whom were illiterate, travelled to Japan
by way of Taiwan or the Philippines. He told me he was paid
$25,000 a trip. When he returned from his third trip, the
Thai Police and Immigration officials were waiting for him,

he said they questioned him for several hours; Sakda produced his briefcase of kid's toys and denied any connection with the running of prostitutes into Japan. He decided to quit after his interrogation, believing he was now under observation by the authorities. I asked him if he felt any remorse about the lives of the females, his fellow citizens he had left behind in Japan; he just shook his head and said, 'What's the fucken difference? Here in Thailand or Japan, they would still be selling their bodies.'

The Chinese have been in Thailand for centuries, sustaining a close relationship through the arts, business and trade, but unlike Indonesia, Malaysia and other South–East Asian nations, the Thai people have co-existed peacefully with the Chinese and there has been much cross-cultural integration over hundreds of years. The Thai-born Chinese or mixed-blood Chinese Thais predominately control the largest businesses, along with the military and governments within Thailand.

CHAPTER 2

MY EIGHTEEN-MONTH CONTRACT FINISHED way too fast. I wasn't ready to return to the cold arctic chill of Canada, so decided to hunt around Thailand for another project. I didn't have long to wait, after a couple of weeks of hanging out in the go-go bars I met an American tourist who worked in the Marine industry. He told me a company in Baltimore, Maryland had just been awarded a contract in Thailand to build a Cutter Suction Dredge for the Royal Thailand Ports and Rivers Authority. This outfit, Eastern Dredging Company, would most likely require an individual to assist with the project in Thailand, so he offered to locate and give me the name and address of the person that I should forward a resume too, which he did a couple of days later.

Several weeks after I had faxed my resume to Baltimore, I received a response, also by fax, advising me that a representative of Eastern Dredging Company, a Mr Smitty, would be at the Royal Orchid Hotel, Bangkok, in several weeks and for me to contact him for an interview appointment.

The Royal Orchid, situated on the banks of the Chao

Phraya River, that twists and turns its way through Bangkok, or Krungthep Maha Nakhon, (the official name of the capital in the Thai language). Bangkok is also known locally as, 'The City of Angles'. The Chao Phraya River or, 'River of Kings', as it is often alluded to in Thai culture, takes its title from Chao Phraya Chakri, King Buddha Yodfa, the first ruler of the Chakri dynasty in Thailand (1782–1809), subsequently referred to as King Rama I.

Numerous piers along the banks of the Chao Phraya River allow travel by express boats, long-tail 'Hang Yoa' ferryboats, hotel shuttle boats and private hire boats.

Earlier in the twentieth century, the Chao Phraya River was the artery, and the klongs (canals), the veins that carried the lifeblood of Bangkok—water. It was not until after World War II that the klongs began to lose importance in a city dubbed by the early settlers from Europe as the 'Venice of the East'. As roads and freeways were constructed, the klongs became less important for passenger transportation, some were filled in, and others were converted into pipelines to drain flood runoff, and concreted over.

Thanks to the long-tail Hang Yoas and their passenger service, several major klongs still continue to alleviate Bangkok traffic congestion.

I travelled the hour and a half by bus from Pattaya City to Bangkok for my six pm interview with this dude Smitty. At the conclusion of my previous project, I had to surrender to my former employer the supplied Isuzu pick-up truck, travel now was by public transport.

I met with Smitty, who turned out to be a friendly guy with a huge walrus-type moustache. We talked about my past experiences and his company's history, which dated back to the construction of the Panama Canal. He told me that his company, Eastern Dredging, had been awarded a contract by the Royal Thailand Ports and Rivers Authority to build one twenty-inch Cutter Suction Dredger; one Tender Boat and a Floating Pipeline for maintenance of shipping channels in and around Bangkok. He added that the Ports and Rivers Authority required another three larger-size Dredgers, and Eastern was trying to secure that project, utilising a local Bangkok agency called Thaitek to assist with the bid process.

He asked me to meet him the following morning for breakfast, after which we would travel to the province of Samutprakarn, which is in reality, an outer suburb of Bangkok heading southeast. This location was where Eastern had formed a joint venture with a local shipyard to build the twenty-inch Dredger, Tender Boat and Pipeline.

After breakfast, Khun Terdsak (In Thailand, the common term utilised for Mr, Mrs, Ms and Miss is 'Khun', pronounced, 'Coon'.) from the Thaitek agency, transported Smitty and me to the Joint Venture Shipyard - Prakarn. Terdsak introduced us to the owners of the Prakarn shipyard, who were an elderly Thai couple in their mid-sixties. Terdsak told me they had been in the shipbuilding industry in and around Bangkok for the past forty years. The yard wasn't much to look at, as they had only just purchased the land and built a small office and workshop; the slipway for vessel launching was under construction.

The old gentleman's name was Khun Savit and he had a business partner to assist him with his shipbuilding program who was a Captain in the Royal Thailand Navy, moonlighting to supplement the low-paying Navy salary. Captain Somboon was a fifty-year-old Naval Architect who had graduated from a university in the city of Ann Arbor, state of Michigan, USA. He spoke fluent English and handled the negotiations with Smitty for the Joint Venture contract on behalf of Prakarn

shipyard. After a long day of contractual discussions, we said
our goodbyes and left the shipyard as the sun was disappear-
ing into the Gulf of Thailand. Smitty paid me a hundred
dollars for my day and advised me that Eastern would hire
me if they won the bid to build the three larger Dredgers.

As for the twenty-inch Dredger project, he would have to
discuss that with his boss on his return to Baltimore and it
would depend on cost margins of the budget, but he would
give it his best shot. I said goodbye to him at his hotel and
hoped we would meet again.

I took a taxi across town to the City Lodge, a cheap joint I
was staying in on Sukhumvit Road, not far from the Ekamai
bus depot where I would catch a bus back to Pattaya City
the next day. As I entered the hotel room I turned on the
TV to channel CNN and hit the shower, as I was drying off I
could hear the female announcer discussing a car accident in
a tunnel in Paris and that Diana had been killed.

I looked at the screen and the lady speaking had puffy red
eyes and looked like she had been crying, I was trying to
think which movie actress had the name Diana but couldn't
come up with a face. I sat on the edge of the bed as the
announcer was discussing the accident with several other TV
personalities. After several minutes, a picture of the wrecked
Mercedes-Benz in the tunnel was shown and a statement was
made of the time and place of the death of Diana, Princess
of Wales.

The following morning I arrived back in Pattaya and took
a Baht bus to the Thai Garden Resort where I was staying. A Baht bus, or Taxi, as they are sometimes called, is
in reality a Japanese manufactured pick-up truck, namely
Isuzu, Nissan or Toyota and in Pattaya, they are mostly all
the same colour—navy blue. The owners, some of whom are
local police and city officials, erect a canopy to cover the box

of the pick-up and install bench seats with a backrest along
both sides. They remove the tailgate and add a few steel steps
to climb aboard; there is an open area between the canopy roof
and walls of the truck box. It can be a pleasant cool ride on
hot days except the traffic fumes flow freely with the breeze,
mostly from diesel-fuelled buses, motor cycles and other pick-
up trucks of which there is an abundance in Pattaya, and of
course when the weather changes to rain, you get wet. Baht
bus drivers have notorious reputations for ripping-off tourists.
When the US Navy hits town for a little R and R, fares have
a strange habit of going from 5 to 500 Baht for the same trip;
drivers often take tourists to shopping-centres, which over-
charge and then they collect 'commissions' from the stores.
Walking along the streets often leads to open solicitation
from the drivers to take tourists for a visit to establishments
with live sex shows and other explicit sexual attractions, some
of the Pattaya visitors are there for that reason only and praise
this service.

I had another three weeks left on my visitor's visa. I had
been to the Thai Immigration office in Pattaya and obtained
a one-month visa extension that had cost 500 Baht. For the
past eighteen months, the company that employed me had
taken care of my visa requirements and work permit, which
was required by all foreigners lawfully employed.

Deportations occur regularly in Thailand, mostly folk
from poorer neighbouring countries like Burma, Laos and
Cambodia who, like the Mexicans in North America, see
opportunities across the borders. However foreigners from
western nations also get tangled up in the immigration police
net and are often classified 'persona non grata'.

After waiting for two weeks and hearing nothing from the
company in Baltimore, I telephoned Smitty and asked him the
status of my possible employment. He told me nothing had

been confirmed yet, as the contract for the three larger Dredgers, which were classified as thirty-inch, had not to date been let. I told him I was running out of visa and would have to renew and to do that I would need to leave the country, plus I would require a letter of intent regarding employment. Under Thailand law, I could receive a three-month non-immigrant visa with this letter. He advised me he would send a fax to Eastern Dredging's agent Thaitek in Bangkok, and have them produce a letter and for me to contact a Dr Pryor—the senior partner of Thaitek. I could then retrieve the letter and go get a visa. This I did and arranged to fly to Singapore.

I was going on a 'Visa Run', as it is known by the local expatriate community in Thailand. When your visa runs out you either leave the country and obtain another tourist visa or you overstay and pay a fine of 200 plus Baht per day, which sometimes inadvertently happens to some folk, the customary alternative being the 'Visa Run'. The most popular, cheapest and closest port for a Thai issuing Consul is Penang, Malaysia, which can be reached by train or bus. You are required to spend twenty–four hours out of Thailand for visa renewal, and usually it is obtainable in Penang in forty–eight hours; however, this depends on time, day and month of your arrival. On occasion, the Thai Consulate personnel in Penang decide that too many visas have been issued to foreigners and if an individual has several renewals in his passport then they will not issue another. This can be a dilemma for some that must then find another location such as Singapore, Jakarta, Kuala Lumpur, Laos or Cambodia. It's crazy but it's the Thai way and most of the visa applicants are male with wives and girlfriends waiting back in Thailand. They will get their visa, even if it means paying an 'under the table commission' or 'tea money' as it is some times called, to an immigration official.

I flew to Singapore and the following morning after my

arrival, I was at the Thailand Embassy on Orchard Road at eight–thirty am, filled out the required documents and submitted them along with my passport, Letter of Employment Intent and forty–six Singapore dollars. Twenty–four hours later, I returned to the Embassy and received my passport with a Non-Immigrant visa that covered one whole page of the passport, valid for three months. The following day I returned to Bangkok's Don Muang airport.

After passing through Thai Immigration and customs without a hitch, I caught a taxi to the office of Eastern's agent Thaitek, which was only a twenty-minute ride from the airport. Parked out front were the Thaitek agency vehicles, several Mercedes-Benz, one BMW and a Saab, in Thailand the saying goes, 'If you got it, flaunt it', obviously Thaitek personnel were no exception to the rule.

The senior partner of Thaitek, Dr Pryor, was the product of a Swiss Father and a Thai Mother, educated mostly in Europe, he received a Doctor of Philosophy at Stanford University in the United States, and his discipline was law. It is customary in Thailand to refer to individuals whom have received a PHD as 'Doctor'.

I climbed the stairs to the second floor of the Thaitek building to the office of Dr Pryor, who was there with his Thai partner, Khun Surasak and two staff members, Terdsak and Khun Preecha. All were in a jubilant mood and quickly informed me they had secured, for Eastern Dredging Company, the three-by-thirty-inch Dredger contract worth $50 million. I congratulated them and listened to the details of how they figured the project would unfold.

Within a week of my return from Singapore, I received a fax from Smitty advising me to meet the owner of Eastern Dredging Co. in Bangkok. Five days later, I once again journeyed to the Royal Orchid Hotel and met the owner and

President, a Mr Edward Brown. According to the Eastern Dredging Company profile, Brown was both Harvard and Yale educated, with that kind of background, you'd think the guy would have some smarts, but there was something distracting about this critter that bothered me. Maybe it was the way he looked at me, that one eye that was not set in its socket square, I was never quite sure if he was looking at me or something behind me, which always gave me the need to turn and look.

After a short discussion, he advised me that we would be going to the US Embassy on Wireless Road where he had an appointment with the Ambassador. The Commercial Attaché met us at the gate of the Embassy's Commercial Section and we were escorted directly to the Ambassador's office; I was asked to wait outside while Brown had his meeting, which lasted about thirty minutes.

At the conclusion of the meeting, we were driven by one of the Thaitek agency staff to the shipyard of the Joint Venture partner where, during a business lunch, the up-coming project was discussed. On the return journey to Brown's hotel, he gave me a copy of an employment contract and advised me to read through it and in a couple of days contact Smitty for discussions.

After several telephone calls and faxes to and from the United States, I received a revised copy of the contract, which I signed and returned it to Smitty.

Several days later, I left for Eastern's head office in Baltimore where I would spend the next six weeks learning Eastern's mindset and meeting the personnel involved with the Thailand project.

CHAPTER 3

O N MY ARRIVAL AT Baltimore Washington International Airport, I took a cab ride to the inner harbour district of downtown Baltimore and checked into the Brookshire Hotel on Lombard Street where Smitty had made reservations for me.

During my first week at Eastern, the Director of Engineering, a guy called Johnson introduced me to all the players involved in the Thailand project from sales, drafting and engineering. Within minutes of meeting Johnson, he told me he was a graduate of the US military academy, West Point, and on every other weekend, he played at being soldier with other weekend warriors. The individual who was the Project Manager for the Thai project, a Mr Rivers, was visiting another Eastern Dredging project in the South East Asian nation of Indonesia and was due to return to Baltimore in several weeks. I was ushered into the office of the Vice President of Human resources, a woman in her mid-forties, whom like most human resource personnel, tended to look down their noses at prospective or new employees and Ms Candy Lawford was no exception.

After several hours of filling in documents with continuous phone call interruptions, Ms Lawford told me that before I returned to Thailand I would be required to sign a company 'confidentiality agreement', which I told her was not a problem.

She displayed many gold baubles on her fingers, arms and neck so I told her that the Thai goldsmiths made exquisite gold jewellery. She asked if I could find a gold neck chain with large links in Thailand, I confirmed I could, and the ensuing discussion was about how the chain could be brought into the United States without her having to pay customs duty.

That same day I met with Smitty and we discussed the forthcoming Thai project. Eastern's contractual obligations with the Thailand Ports and Rivers Authority was to build the three by thirty-inch cutter suction Dredges, three Tender Boats, and three thirty-inch diameter Floating Pipelines in the United States. However, Eastern's intention was to have all the equipment built in the Kingdom of Thailand and the following day Smitty would fly to Bangkok to meet with the representatives of a Thai shipyard and pursue negotiations for a contract to build all items in their Bangkok facilities. The shipyard in question was South Asia Shipping Co., located almost opposite the Joint Venture Shipyard-Prakarn, on the Chao Phaya River, which dissects the common province of Sumutprakarn.

During the next six weeks of my visit with Eastern, I met and spoke with all the people involved with the Thailand project. One individual, Jimmy Churchill, a naval architect from the United Kingdom, who had been living and working in the United States for more than twenty years, enlightened me about Eastern Dredging. He advised me to be sure that I had everything I required for my contract in Thailand in writing, as anything stated or promised verbally would not happen, additionally, to be on guard about receiving salary and expenses as Eastern management often delayed payments. He also told me that the guy Eastern had hired and was stationed on the Indonesian project was owed more than $20,000 in unpaid expenses. He was in a continuing battle for his money.

I responded that from all the accolades, patents, photographs of Dredges, and worldwide projects that were covering most of the office building wall space—Eastern seemed to have been a strong company in the past.

'Yes, and that's about all they have,' he said, 'a past, and it's all hanging on the walls, so be careful.' He continued that at month's end he was leaving Eastern, as he could no longer work with some of the other employees.

One in particular, Ted, who had the title of 'Engineering Manager', had never attended a college or university, consequently he never had a degree, however, he had worked at Eastern for the past thirty years and had been trained as a draftsman. Churchill said the guy was a terrible backstabber and a two-faced, motherfucken liar to boot, he added that he refused to attend any meeting where draftsman Ted, as he called him, was present and he also refused to speak to the guy.

Seems the six years that Churchill had been with Eastern, these two guys had crossed swords on many occasions. He also told me that the Director of Engineering, the 'weekend warrior' Johnson, who had only been with Eastern eight months—had been responsible for draftsman Ted being promoted to his current status, passing over degreed and competent Engineers with many years of service to Eastern. As I met and spoke with some of the Engineers regarding the Thailand project, it was not difficult to recognise animosity that existed within the Engineering department. I had several discussions with both draftsman Ted and the weekend warrior Johnson regarding the Thai project. Although they were courteous and answered my questions, it was Ted who had the knowledge regarding the blueprint drawings of the Dredges, but then after thirty years he should have. I guessed Johnson allied himself with Ted to sustain his own inadequacies, as prior to joining Eastern he had been an adviser to a US government Arms contractor selling military armoured tanks to the Egyptian government.

After several weeks of being in Baltimore, Rivers, the project manager for Thailand, arrived back from Indonesia and Thailand where he had been in negotiations with Smitty in Bangkok regarding the hiring of a Thai shipyard, he told me that during my absence from Thailand the economic and political climate was changing rapidly.

When I had first arrived in Thailand mid 1994, the Thai Baht was valued at twenty–five to one American dollar. When I left to visit Baltimore in October 1997, it was thirty–two to one American dollar and falling, by November it was down to thirty–nine and still heading south.

The preceding months had seen two Prime Ministers come and go and the third, Chuan Leek Pai, take over as an interim government, trying to arrest the economic crisis and prevent Thailand from going completely down the tubes. Chuan had been Prime Minister in 1994.

However, after elections, which were heavily controlled by vote-buying and political assassinations, the new Prime Minister, Banharn, a so-called Chinese Thai whose origins and educational qualifications became questionable, had to step down when it became evident that his government was devastating Thailand's economy. Before departing, one of his long remembered statements after being accused of accepting an under the table commission of four million US dollars by an Indian-born fugitive financier (who had been a consultant to the now defunct Bangkok Bank of Commerce) was, "If you meet a cobra snake and an Indian together, kill the Indian first." Another big spender and vote buyer replaced Banharn—a retired Army General named Chavalit, whose reign of corruption and mismanagement was short lived and Thailand was once more placed in the hands of Chuan Leek Pai. Respected by the majority of Thais, Chuan's reputation was that of the least corruptible of all senior politicians. However, it was basically impossible for this Prime Minister to surround himself with honest ministers, and the country's currency continued to slide until it reached fifty–two to the American dollar. In mid 1998, it bottomed out and began to hold and slowly climb upwards to forty and then later to thirty–seven by Christmas 1998.

Smitty returned to Baltimore mid November from Bangkok bringing with him a signed agreement with the Thai shipyard, South Asia Shipping Co. (Sasco), to build the Dredges, Tender Boats and Pipeline for the price of $19 million. Involved with the contract was a demarcation list of equipment. The Dredges required dual Caterpillar engines connected in tandem to drive the huge Dredge hull pumps, hydraulic systems, and cutter suction systems, as well as piping for fuel and engine water-cooling systems. Another Caterpillar engine would be installed for electrical and instrumentation systems. The demarcation list was utilised to divide the supplying of equipment for each system between Eastern and the shipyard, the majority of which would be Eastern's responsibility.

The equipment would be purchased in the United States and sea-freighted to the shipyard in Thailand for installation. According to the project manager, this still left a profit of many millions of dollars for Eastern.

I hung around Baltimore for another couple of weeks having meetings with the project manager, Rivers and Smitty regarding the Thai project.

I told them that even though they had experience with projects in Indonesia and Vietnam, the Thai people were completely different from other Asians and the one thing that should not be forgotten that sets Thais apart from all their other South–East Asian neighbours, is the fact that Thailand has never been colonised. Many nations had tried, Burma, China, France, England and even the United States with its dollars, battles were fought but the Thais were not to be beaten, and I quoted the last couple of lines of the Thai National Anthem, *"All Thais are ready to give up every drop of blood for the nation's safety, freedom and progress"*.

I had spent many years working with Singaporeans, Filipinos, and Indonesians and had learned that in Thailand, like nowhere else, there is only one way that things get done, and that is the 'Thai Way' or 'Thai Style'. You can explain, you can demonstrate, but the Thai psyche stands firm, they do things their way and the best you can do is stand by and try to guide things. If you doublecross or cheat them, look out, because they do believe in revenge. I had also on several occasions informed Eastern's owner, Brown, of the Thai formula, however no one took me seriously, and I guessed they figured they knew it all; well it was up to them.

During my first assignment in Thailand, I met an Australian sales representative for welding equipment; Mal had lived in Thailand in excess of ten years and was married to a Thai lady. During our initial conversation, Mal told me a story regarding a plant manager that had been imported from Australia to improve the production and quality of a local manufacturing company. Mal told me the guy was a loud and aggressive individual—the wrong approach in Asia, or most anywhere for that matter, anyhow one evening he locked up his office and left for the day. On his return the next morning, he unlocked the office door, entered and sat down behind his desk. Standing upright on his writing pad on the desk was a nine mm bullet, no windows or the door to the office had been forced, according to Mal the Aussie put the bullet into a desk drawer and went about his daily business. That evening, the same procedure—lock up the office and leave for the day. The following morning, same routine, unlocks the office, enters and sits behind his desk, and there again on the desktop was an upright nine mm bullet, again no forced entry into the office. However this second morning was different, less than fifteen minutes after his arrival at the office his telephone rang and a male voice speaking English with a Thai accent gave him a simple message, 'The second bullet is for your wife'. Apparently, the guy was on the next plane heading home. I wasn't sure but I guessed Mal had given me a serious insight into the Land of Smiles.

During the mid nineties, numerous projects in the Petrochemical industry were under construction on the Thai Eastern Seaboard. Within the Maptaput industrial zone of Rayong province, Shell Oil and Caltex Petroleum Co. were building oil refineries, while other Japanese, Korean and American companies were expanding their chemical and petroleum plants. One Korean outfit had imported its own supervisors from Korea for the construction of a chemical plant in the industrial complex. Koreans have a terrible reputation of abusing their subordinates, one of these supervisors made the mistake of slapping, on several occasions, a few of the Thai workers under his supervision. Almost predictably, the Korean went missing; his pick-up truck was found several hundred kilometres to the east of Maptaput parked at a Buddhist Temple near the Thai Cambodian border. The unfortunate, but foolish Korean was discovered in a roadside ditch not far from the project site, he had been shot at close range through the head. Police investigations learned that the Thai workers on the Korean project had pooled their salaries and hired a local police officer to assassinate the Korean.

The cop was arrested and is doing time in the local 'Monkey House', as Thais refer to a prison. He will probably obtain a Royal Pardon in the not-too-distant future though, as on the King of Thailand's birthday each year many prisoners are released, and under the circumstances of this killing, as it was in the interest of the Thai people who were being abused by a foreigner, release is imminent.

The Eastern Dredging Company issued me with a laptop computer, I had told Smitty I would pay for it, as I needed a personal computer, he said it could be arranged and to speak with the project manager Rivers which I did. 'Hell,' he said, 'don't worry about it, when the project is over it's yours.'

That evening after we had finished work, Rivers drove me back to the hotel, on the way he told me that he had friends who owned a Marine Diesel-Electric company in Texas and from time to time, he would use them for consulting work on Eastern Dredge projects. By doing this he had set up a 'Slush Fund' meaning, he would have them invoice Eastern over and above their account and the excess was his. He told me that he would be able to send me, from time to time, a little extra compensation from this 'fund', I thanked him and said goodbye as the following day I flew back to Bangkok.

CHAPTER 4

O N ARRIVAL INTO BANGKOK at midnight, I hired an airport limo and was driven to the southeastern suburb of Bangna, and the Novotel Hotel. I had been assured by Smitty that Eastern's agent, Thaitek had made reservations, but on arrival—no reservations; fortunately they had vacancies even though it was the beginning of the tourist high season.

Over the following weeks, I located and rented a two-bedroom condominium. My contract also stated 350,000 Baht ($10,000) for a vehicle to be made available by Eastern at the time of contract signing. However, by the time Eastern finally trans-ferred the dollar equivalent of 350,000, the Baht was fifty–two to one US dollar, equating to $6,730, which meant a vehicle of the quality that I had expected would not be purchased. Any-how, I located and bought a two-year-old Isuzu pick-up truck. I had assumed the agent Thaitek would register the vehicle in their company name but they refused, I tried to have the truck registered in the Joint Venture's company name but they too refused. The reason for refusal was that in Thailand, no matter who is driving a vehicle, if it is involved in an accident the owner must pay for damages. So if a foreigner is driving and a Thai is involved in the accident, all that the Thai will see is a large sack of money, a wallet with legs, regardless of insurance. Obviously, neither Thaitek nor the Joint Venture folk wanted any involvement. I informed Rivers of the conundrum; his only solutions was register it in your name.

There is a saying among foreign drivers living in Thailand, 'if you drive in Thailand you have one foot on the accelerator and the other foot in a Thai jail'. During my stay in Pattaya City, it was not uncommon for a Thai to deliberately ram a vehicle driven by a foreigner with his own machine to obtain a cash settlement. If the police were involved, they always sided with their fellow countryman, advising the foreigner, 'if you were not in Thailand the accident would not have happened'. The police always offered to escort the foreign victim to the nearest ATM machine. To prevent jail time, all parties must be paid off. Several foreigners had the experience of the police persuasive tactic of producing their service revolvers to encourage the ATM visit.

In Thailand, a foreigner can buy a vehicle and have a driver's licence but unless you have a one-year visa you can't register the vehicle in your own name, fortunately I had organised and received a twelve-month visa and work permit. In my previous experience of working in Thailand and overseas in many countries, visa and work permits had always been the employer's responsibility and were provided. However, when it came to Eastern Dredging Co. I was on my own, and their agent Thaitek did not feel that they were obliged to assist, referring to their contract with Eastern. I hired a Thai lawyer and paid him well, passing on the costs in my monthly expenses, which I learned I had to fight for, as Churchill had told me back in Baltimore.

After renting the condo and buying the Isuzu, I began visiting the two shipyards. The Joint Venture yard where the one twenty-inch cutter suction Dredge was to be built, was twenty kilometres from the condo, the Sasco yard which was contracted to build the three, thirty-inch cutter suction Dredgers was forty kilometres in the opposite direction. Although both shipyards were in the province of Samutprakarn and sat almost opposite each other on the banks of the Chao Phraya River, I had to drive twenty kilometres and cross the river via the majestic Rama IX Bridge, then double back to get to Sasco's yard. The bridge was built in 1987 to celebrate His Majesty the King's fifth cycle and is the world's longest single-plane cable-stayed bridge with an overall length of three kilometres. That route took me through the notorious suburb of Prapadang, which entertains seamen from around the world fulfilling their wildest fantasies while their ships are moored along the docks of the Chao Phraya.

Samutprakarn province has its own historical notoriety for political corruption; during a recent election, 10,000 candidates competed for just 200 seats, many election hopefuls and canvassers equipped themselves with firearms and bulletproof vests in anticipation of violence during the election. Further controversy regarding the integrity of the province, involved allegations of trading in human organs. The allegations stated that certain hospitals were working in a syndicate to monitor patients in a terminal condition and then asking their families to sell their kidneys for use in transplants, despite knowing it was illegal. Disclosure of the active kidney for-sale business came to light after a father's complaint that a hospital took kidneys from his daughter without his permission and offered him money after her death. The Thai Red Cross Society, which is the sole agency authorised to control kidney donations, exposed that kidneys were being

27

removed from the dead poor and sold to live rich patients. The Thailand Medical Council launched investigations into these horrendous activities.

To enable Eastern to be awarded the contract for the thirty-inch Dredges, a bid bond of two million dollars was required. Eastern was strapped for cash and asked Sasco's owner, Khun Mechi, if he could assist. Owner Mechi and his yard Managing Director and nephew, Khun Chang, immediately approached their bank and within forty–eight hours had a letter of credit covering the amount. The United States Trade and Development Agency of Washington, DC offered the Thailand Ports and Rivers Authority a grant of $400,000 to support its training activities on the condition that the Ports and Rivers Authority awarded the contract to Eastern. The agency offered the Ports and Rivers Authority an opportunity to design a training program to meet their objectives, which could include simulator-based harbour pilot training, navigational-aid training, oil-spill training, studies related to environmental aspects of dredging and several other programs with the US Coast Guard, and the US Army Corps of Engineers.

Director General Vanchai of the Ports and Rivers Authority and his bid committee agreed and the contract was awarded to Eastern.

Four days later, Director General Vanchai was transferred to the Environmental Department and his committee was disbanded and transferred to different departments within the Ports and Rivers Authority. A new Director General, Allrot, took the reins and formed an inspection committee, which would oversee the two Dredger projects, no one was sure why—TiT.

As Eastern's engineering of the Dredges progressed, technical changes occurred. Before these changes could be implemented, documentation explaining why these changes were necessary had to be presented to the Ports and Rivers Authority Inspection Committee. As I was a newcomer regarding the required procedures of presentation, I required assistance from Thaitek. I visited their office on a regular basis receiving guidance from their junior rep who was also their accountant. Preecha was a Chinese Thai, about five feet six inches and weighing in at a hundred pounds soaking wet, who spoke fractured English.

Dr Pryor, Thaitek's senior partner had no problem with the English language and spoke to me about monies he claimed his company had paid to members of the Ports and Rivers Authority as under the table commission, which enabled Eastern to win the contract. He required reimbursement from Eastern, and asked that I pass the message to Smitty, who would then pass the request on to Eastern's owner Brown.

The Joint Venture Shipyard ordered steel plate to commence building the twenty-inch Dredge hull, but would not start construction until they received approved blueprint drawings from the Ports and Rivers Authority. Meanwhile, Sasco had ordered and was having steel plate shipped to Bangkok from Singapore, scheduling a 'keel lay' ceremony during the second week after Christmas.

In the Land of Smiles, Christmas is not a date of consequence, as it has no significance for the majority of Thai Buddhists or the minority of Thai Muslims. However, 'Happy New Year' is celebrated, not once but three times a year in Thailand—Western New Year that begins on January 1st, Chinese New Year, which occurs the end of January or beginning of February and April 13th the Thai New Year or 'Songkran', as it is called.

The Songkran festival is one of the oldest in Thailand and celebrates the South Asian lunar New Year. Celebrated in India, it was adopted by neighbouring countries such as Cambodia, Burma, Laos and Thailand. The literal meaning of Songkran is 'to move from one place to another'; this is in reference to the earth revolving around the sun. The complete circumference, of course, is the universal marking of a New Year.

The ancient Thai calendar is divided into twelve months. The lunar Thai year begins with the month of April. Taking the years in a cycle of twelve, the Thai and Chinese calendars are defined by unique animals, each year having a certain predicted characteristic. In the West, the year is taken in a cycle of twelve months and each month has a certain predicted characteristic based on the astrological computations of each month.

During the reign of King Rama V, of Thailand, a great compromise was reached. The King wanted to bridge the differences in the Thai and Western calendars. This wise King saw the need for a unified calendar to facilitate commerce between East and West. Therefore, if one looks at a Thai calendar, it is divided into twelve months and three hundred and sixty–five days, which is the same as the calendars of the West. The year, however, is different. The Thai year reflects the year of Buddha, which is five hundred and forty–three years older than the Christian calendar. If you are looking at a Thai Calendar, you must subtract five hundred and forty–three from the year for the current western calendar year. The year 2000 is the Thai year 2543 or the Chinese year of the Dragon. King Rama V changed the calendar but explained to the Thai people that the calendar did not change their celebration. April 13th would always be the Thai New Year.

The celebration of Songkran for Thailand is actually a very gentle and beautiful expression of love and respect. Tourists visiting Thailand during the Thai New Year are familiar with the water and talcum powder that is thrown by the bucket-full, but this is not the true Thai celebration.

There are four parts to the Thai New Year celebration. Because the Thais hold the family in such great respect, all the family joins together either at a Buddhist temple or at the home of one of the family members and participates in the four parts of the Songkran celebration. The first is to 'make merit'. Special food is prepared and given to the monks in respect for their position as teachers of the Buddhist doctrines.

This offering to the monks usually takes place in the morning. The second part of the celebration is the bathing of the statue of Buddha. The Buddha is honoured by bathing with clean water scented with rose and jasmine. The third part of the celebration is honouring the elders of the family, such as the grandparents and aunts and uncles. Clean scented water is gently poured over the hands of the honoured person. As the water is poured, the family prays for the health and happiness of each person.

The family shares in a feast of delicacies that has been prepared with great care, not only for the taste but also for presentation. Beautifully carved fruit is arranged among the various dishes to please the eye as well as the taste buds. The fourth and last part of the celebration is the prayers offered toward their ancestors, loved ones and honoured teachers or advisors. The Thai Buddhists do not bury their dead but cremate them and small portions of the ashes are reserved for traditional ceremonies. During the Songkran celebration, the family uses these small portions of the reserved ashes to pray and show respect for the memory of those departed.

The New Year rolled around and the Joint Venture was still waiting for approved drawings and would not accept steel delivery until the drawings were received. However, Sasco shipyard was hard at work, the northern section of their yard was being levelled and concrete was poured. A steel fabrication workshop was being built, as was a slipway for launching the Dredges. Steel had arrived and was being placed at three locations on concrete blocks to be welded together to form the three keels for the three-by-thirty-inch Dredges. A keel lay ceremony was scheduled and Sasco requested a list of personnel who would be attending from Eastern and its agent Thaitek. I discussed the keel lay situation with Smitty and Rivers; some kind of problem seemed to be developing between those turkeys. Rivers informed me that maybe the weekend warrior Johnson would be assuming Smitty's duties. I hoped this would not occur as Smitty had it together regarding Thailand and all the parties concerned. Early January I telephoned Smitty and he told me he would not be returning to Thailand until the end of the month, which meant he would not be attending the keel lay ceremony.

Later I telephoned the Project Manager Rivers, he added that no one from the Baltimore office would be in attendance. It would be just Thaitek personnel and myself.

Sasco had worked at welding the plates to form the three keels, twenty–four hours a day for the previous three days to meet the schedule.

The end user of the Dredges, the Royal Thailand Ports and Rivers Authority, had not yet approved Sasco as a shipyard to build the Dredges and therefore they would not be represented at the ceremony. Sasco were taking a risk by forging ahead with the project before approval but they were confident it would soon be received. After all, they had a signed agreement with Eastern, and Eastern had a signed contract with the Ports and Rivers Authority and had received $7.5 million down payment at the completion of contract documentation. Additionally, the new Director General Allrot of the

Ports and Rivers Authority had, years earlier, been a paid consultant to Sasco and he and MD Chang were supposedly close friends.

By the second week in January, the area around the three keels was as clean and shiny as a new penny, Sasco had erected a large tent and seating arrangements for some thirty-odd people was set-up. Nine Buddhist monks were in attendance and they chanted their ritual, which lasted for about half an hour, flower petals and holy water were then sprinkled on the three keels. It was then my turn to press the button and fire up three electric arc-welding machines, which simulated arc welding of the keels for several minutes.

Other than the Buddhist monks, Sasco personnel and myself were the only attendees, Thaitek personnel never showed even tho they had assured me the previous day they would. Before the ceremony commenced, the shipyard MD Chang approached me, spoke about Eastern's agent, Thaitek, stating he did not believe they were doing their job, and were negligent regarding obtaining approval of Sasco shipyard from the Ports and Rivers Authority. He also said that Smitty, as project Engineer, should be in Bangkok and applying pressure to assist with the approval. The following day I told Thaitek's Dr Pryor about MD Chang's assessment of what Thaitek was or was not doing. Pryor lost his cool and stated he would tell MD Chang to quit shooting his mouth off, but as the saying goes, 'talk is cheap'.

CHAPTER 5

EVERY YEAR SINCE 1982, except for 1991 when the United States cancelled in protest because of a military coup, a joint US–Thai military exercise known as 'Cobra Gold' is usually held during the month of May. The February 1991 coup toppled the democratically elected government of Prime Minister Chatichai Choonhavan, allowing military strongman General Suchinda to wield power and in the following months manipulate Thai politics such that by 1992 he had himself appointed Prime Minister. Pro-democracy demonstrators protesting against what they described as an illegitimate rise to power created massive street protests. Clashes erupted as the government declared a state of emergency and warned the media against reporting or publishing pictures, which could influence civil unrest. Under direct orders from Prime Minister General Suchinda, military officers ordered troops to open fire on the demonstrators—killing thousands. This bloody incident has become known throughout Thailand as 'Black May', the protesters who lost their lives in the pro-democracy fight have gone down in Thai history as the 'May Heroes'. After three days of violence and bloodshed, the country's political path was drastically altered forever.

The US–Thai war games injected approximately ten million US dollars into the Thai economy, which in 1998 was in shambles. The International Monetary Fund and World Bank personnel were flying in and out of Bangkok for meetings with the Thai government on a regular basis, trying to stabilise the economy and arrest the domino affect on other Asian Nations' economies unsuccessfully.

By the end of January, Smitty, the weekend warrior Johnson, and Eastern's owner Brown arrived at the Royal Orchid Hotel. I had a discussion with all three regarding the finalisation of a shipyard to build the Dredgers; the consensus from their point of view was that MD Chang of Sasco was a shithead, I wasn't sure how they had reached this conclusion and Thaitek's Dr Pryor stated, 'Chang wasn't worth worrying about'. The following day I accompanied Smitty and the weekend warrior to the office of Captain Chitepong, retired Thailand Navy (RTN), chairman of the twenty-inch Dredger inspection committee at the Ports and Rivers Authority.

The discussion was cordial and genial until the weekend warrior contradicted a statement by Smitty, whereupon it escalated into sarcasm; both Captain Chitepong and myself were surprised to say the least. After a few minutes, everything was back to normal and we left Chitepong's office. I didn't say anything but thought the sarcasm had gone over like a fart in church. For these guys to disagree in front of Chitepong represented a 'Loss of Face' in Thai culture, and it was not good.

The following day we all met with Director General Allrot of the Ports and Rivers Authority, Brown discussed Sasco shipyard approval and technical items for both projects. I was issued a letter for Power of Attorney, allowing me to sign off technical items on behalf of and for Eastern.

Several meetings were slated with the Ports and Rivers Authority but never occurred, however, a dinner meeting was arranged with the Sasco shipyard at the oldest and grandest hotel in Bangkok, 'The Oriental'. It was an outside affair under huge trees decorated with small white twinkling lights on a large concrete balcony with a two-foot high concrete wall abutting the Chao Praya River, a magnificent location. Sasco was in full representation with the presence of the Owner, Managing Director, General Manager and Executive Technical Manager. All participants were civil and the buffet meal was excellent. At the conclusion of the evening, Smitty took me to one side and told me to meet him and the weekend warrior Johnson, at another Bangkok shipyard called Roma Thai Marine the following morning, he and Johnson would take a taxi from the Hotel. I told him okay, but that I didn't understand why, which he said he would explain tomorrow.

Roma Thai Marine shipyard is no doubt one of the best-equipped yards in Thailand, which includes a floating dry dock. Smitty and weekend warrior Johnson were already at the yard when I arrived, they had with them a full set of blueprint drawings for the three thirty-inch Dredgers and were seated in the yard-manager's office discussing the building of the Dredgers. As I listened to the conversation after introductions, I realised that these turkeys were requesting a bid proposal regarding the construction of the Dredgers from RomaThai Marine.

As we were escorted on an inspection review of the yard, Smitty informed me that if the three by thirty-inch Dredger project was to be removed from Sasco, Thailand, to the United States that he, Smitty, had advised Brown that I should remain with the project and go with it to the US. I really couldn't believe what I was being told, saying to Smitty that it was my understanding that Eastern had an agreement with Sasco and all we needed was Ports and Rivers Authority approval. Hell, the keels were already laid and Sasco had almost completed the workshop and slipway and that was costing a bunch of money, which they hoped to recoup with the Dredger project.

Smitty's response was, 'Well Brown thinks their price is too high and he is talking about either retrieving part of it or all of it.' I was amazed at this statement and reminded Smitty that he had better warn Brown that the Thais were not like other Asians and if he pulled shit like that, there was no way he would walk away unscathed or wealthy, one way or another they would nail his ass.

Later that afternoon we had a meeting with Sasco's technical people at their shipyard, along with Smitty, the weekend Warrior Johnson and myself. During the meeting once again the hostility between Smitty and Johnson flared, the Sasco people and I sat in embarrassed silence until the air cleared.

As the meeting progressed, Smitty excused himself and stated he had another meeting at the Royal Orchid Hotel with the management of the Joint Venture partnership and he departed—another 'Loss of Face' in front of the Thais. Brown was to have joined the meeting but he had left Thailand the previous night. According to him, he had been appointed by the Vice President of the United States, Al Gore, to be a member of the Young Presidents organisation and he had to attend a meeting between the export business leaders in Egypt and other members of the Young Presidents club.

After the meeting as I drove the thirty minutes from Sasco shipyard to the Royal Orchid Hotel with the weekend warrior Johnson, his total conversation concerned Smitty and how he was a no good, un-knowledgeable, useless fuckwit, who lacked basic engineering skills, this continued until we were almost at the hotel. I had put the old brain on automatic pilot, mumbling yes, no and okay responses until finally I said to him, 'Well this guy you are calling a dumb stupid Motherfucker is the same guy that hired me, so where does that leave me?'

Johnson went silent for a moment, and then said, 'Well that's the only thing he's done right on this project.' I often thought that maybe I'd gotten lost in the shuffle of life, now I was beginning to wonder if I wasn't shuffling along with the lost!

The following day we had an official meeting with the Ports and Rivers Authority's twenty-inch Inspection Committee. Present were Smitty, Johnson and myself along with six committee members who were all wearing Rolex watches, designer shirts, ties and tailor made suits of expensive cloth, several were even sporting diamond rings. I knew that the average public service salary for their level of expertise was approximately 35,000 to 45,000 Baht per month, with the current exchange rate that would mean $673 to $865 per month. I also knew that the chairman owned and drove a Mercedes-Benz while his co-chairman was the proud owner of a BMW 3231A, which cost more than two million Baht. I wasn't sure how these guys came by their wealth but guessed it was either by coming from wealthy families; accepting many under the table commissions or both. But then corruption, bribes, under the table commissions and tea money are all a fact of Thai society; hell during the Thailand economic boom years of the nineties, a couple of enterprising executives and their treasury advisor at the now defunct Bangkok Bank of Commerce, utilised 'top executive privilege' to misappropriate forty billion Baht. These turkeys had set up more than one hundred and forty companies using unskilled and uneducated labourers as directors and executives of the companies, most of the billions were funnelled through the companies as loans and then into offshore accounts belonging to these assbags. Of course, this did not go unnoticed and currently all three are doing time in the 'Monkey House'.

During the meeting with the Inspection committee, discussions regarding technical items and drawing approvals were going smoothly until the weekend warrior Johnson spoke up very loud and strong, telling the committee that he was the Director of Engineering. Back in Baltimore, he had twenty–five engineers and draftsmen working on this project, and whatever technical items needed changing would be changed for the betterment of the Dredge. Nothing wrong with that statement, but in Thailand your tone of voice and speaking loud in a demanding manner, is, in the eyes of the Thai people, 'Losing Face' and they say any person who conducts themselves in this manner is, 'Ting Tong', which translates into being somewhat fucken nutty.

After the meeting adjourned, we all walked the several hundred yards from the Ports and Rivers Authority building to the Royal Orchid Hotel for lunch, which consisted of the four basic flavours of Thai cooking—sour, sweet, creamy and salty plus heat. Later in the afternoon I was alone with Smitty in his room discussing the meeting and technical items of concern, when Johnson entered and aggressively spoke to Smitty, saying that in his opinion Smitty had fucked up the project and that all we were doing, because of Smithy's lack of knowledge, was playing catch-up. Briefly, I thought he was going to get physical, but he stormed out of the room saying, 'That's it, to hell with you!'

I was reporting by fax and telephone daily to the Project Manager Rivers. When I told him about the Smitty/Johnson episodes his only response was that, he wasn't surprised.

Several more meetings occurred with the Ports and Rivers Authority and Sasco, all concerning engineering technical items and obtaining Ports and Rivers Authority approval of Sasco shipyard to build the Dredges. I was continuously hearing that it should only take 'several more days'. Smitty showed me a letter that had been placed under his hotel-room door. It was from the weekend warrior, telling Smithy that, 'If he questioned him about technical items, or asked him if he understood the items regarding the project when they were in company, then he, Johnson, would terminate the conversation immediately. Also if Smitty pointed a finger at the engineering department regarding any issue then there would be ten fingers pointing right back at Smitty.' Man this shit was getting crazy.

Several days later, both Smitty and the weekend warrior Johnson left for Baltimore, however Johnson's flight departed six hours before Smitty's. I guess they had their reasons for not travelling together.

Another month rolled around, strange noises were emerging across the telephone and fax line out of Baltimore. I received verbal instructions from Smitty to submit to the Ports and Rivers Authority several engineering technical items for the inspection committee's approval, including the contractual payment terms. The following day Rivers, the Project Manager informed me that Brown was pissed off that the contractual payment terms document had been submitted to the committee. It seemed to me that in Baltimore the left hand didn't always know what the right hand was doing. I decided that all future submittals would require written instructions. Rivers also asked me if I would be interested in subcontracting the three Floating Pipelines, in other words, I would hire a contractor to fabricate the Pipelines, oversee the project and pocket ten to fifteen percent of the total cost, which was worth approximately $2 million. I responded that of course I would be interested. I mean, for that chunk of change—$200,000 to $300,000, who wouldn't be? After all, 'living well is the best revenge'. Rivers said he would be in Bangkok within the next couple of weeks and we would discuss it further.

Several days later, I received a couriered package from Baltimore. It contained a demarcation list of items that Eastern would supply and what items the contractor would supply with regards to building the three by thirty-inch Dredges.

The package also contained instructions advising me, 'The demarcation list was to be delivered to the RomaThai Marine shipyard under strict secrecy.' Things were now turning to bullshit.

I also received via the Internet, a 'cc' copy of an email from Sasco shipyard to Eastern. Seems Sasco had smelled a rat and were asking why their shipyard hadn't been named in some contractual documents, which had passed from Brown to the Ports and Rivers Authority. Also that they, Sasco, were in contact with a law firm in Baltimore and in Bangkok and would, if the circumstances did not alter, pursue the matter in court. Rivers telephoned and advised me to cease visiting the Sasco shipyard. I was beginning to wonder if I shouldn't start watching the rear-view mirrors for any sign of two guys on a black unmarked motorcycle!

CHAPTER 6

S EVERAL DAYS LATER, I visited Thaitek's office and
parked the pale blue Isuzu pick-up out front between
the Mercedes-Benz, BMWs, Jeep Grand Cherokees and
Saabs then headed for Dr Pryor's office on the second floor.

The building contained five floors, a travel agency owned
and operated by Pryor's wife occupied the ground floor. The
two things that were always noticeable when I walked through
the front door was the pretty smiling faces of the young Thai
girls that assisted Pryor's wife and the odour—the closest
description of the smell would have to be day-old dog shit. I
always wondered why it didn't seem to bother them, but then,
there are an abundance of odours throughout Bangkok.

After saying hello, Dr Pryor immediately launched into a
prolonged bout of verbal diarrhoea regarding non-contrac-
tual-payments from Eastern Dredging Company, and he was
extremely agitated that Eastern had not reimbursed him
for the monies he claimed to have paid as under the table
commissions to the original Ports and Rivers Authority Bid
committee.

Thaitek's contract with Eastern was for $2,550,000 to be paid immediately upon Eastern's receipt of the project down-payment, Eastern agreed to pay Thaitek fifteen percent of all money received from the Ports and Rivers Authority as 'change orders' or 'extras' on either the twenty-inch or the thirty-inch contracts. Thaitek was also to obtain, on behalf of Eastern, a delivery extension approval by the Ports and Rivers Authority for three months or more, preferably more. Thaitek was to obtain approval of Sasco as subcontractor without reduction in the contract price to Eastern Dredging Co.

They also had a service agreement with Eastern that paid them $50,000 per month; this was for ongoing project services such as meeting with Ports and Rivers Authority and Thai government officials and settling any disputes that may occur, and making under the table commission payments.

Pryor also informed me that Sasco people had visited with Director General Allrot, complaining of Brown's dirty tricks, and the Inspection Committee had reached a decision where they would cease all activities regarding the processing of documentation for the thirty-inch Dredger project because Eastern had incorrectly addressed all documents submitted to the Committee Chairman. This had been done on the advice of the BMW-driving, Rolex-watch-and-diamond-ring-wearing committee vice-chairman, Piboon, now all documents had to be withdrawn and resubmitted to the attention of the Director General.

Because of irregularities in documents signed and submitted by Eastern's owner Brown, and because of the absence of Sasco being listed as the designated shipyard in Thailand, no approval by the Ports and Rivers Authority could be granted until this situation was rectified.

That evening I spoke by telephone to both Smitty and

Rivers, neither seemed to be disturbed and they told me that Brown was the boss and it was up to him. Rivers told me to call the shipyard, RomaThai Marine, and ask them to lower their bid price of $7.5 million and to go ahead and write bid request letters and forward them along with sets of Floating Pipeline drawings to fabricating companies in Thailand for construction costs. He ended by saying he would arrive in Bangkok within the next couple of days. Seemed to me Brown had decided to quit the Sasco agreement and shop the project around town.

After arriving at RomaThai Marine shipyard, I met with the yard manager, who told me that MD Chang, of Sasco had telephoned him and discussed the thirty-inch Dredger project. Chang stated he had a signed agreement with Eastern and as far as he was concerned if the Dredgers were going to be built in Thailand, it would only happen in his yard.

There were no secrets in Thailand when it involved actions and movements of foreigners doing business; it was like living in a fish bowl. Also the local Thai shipyards belonged to an organisation called the 'Thailand Shipbuilders Association' and I guessed the word was on the street that a lucrative project was swinging in the wind and economic times were tough. I also spoke with the yard manager regarding Rivers' request of lowering the bid price; his response was, 'If we get the project the offer can be lowered.'

I left RomaThai Marine shipyard and drove the fifteen kilometres to the Joint Venture Shipyard - Prakarn, dodging a multitude of stray dogs along the way. The owner Khun Savit told me, through his interpreter—as he spoke about as much English as I spoke Thai, which didn't allow for much conversation—that the steel plates for the twenty-inch Dredger would arrive at his yard in a week or so and building would commence almost immediately.

If ever a country was to be recognised for an abundance of abandoned domestic animals Thailand with its huge population of stray mongrel bred dogs would take first place.

Dogs of all types roam and fornicate with abundance and die daily by the hundreds, some starving and badly flea-bitten, some of old age but most are scattered along the streets and highways, victims of unexpected road kill. Woven into the social fabric of Thai Buddhism and Thai culture is a belief of reincarnation and also the belief that the dog is particularly effective in repulsing evil sprits, because of these beliefs, dogs are never voluntarily killed.

The morning after Rivers arrived in Bangkok, I picked him up from the Royal Orchid Hotel and we drove to RomaThai Marine shipyard for further contractual discussions with the yard manager. During the discussions, the manager told us he had received another telephone call from Sasco's MD Chang, who had informed him that Eastern's agent Thaitek had submitted the RomaThai Marine shipyard to the Ports and Rivers Authority as an alternative Thai shipyard to build the Dredges.

He told us MD Chang was pissed off big time and again reiterated that his shipyard, Sasco, had a signed agreement with Eastern and there was only one shipyard in Thailand that was going to build the Dredges and it wasn't RomaThai Marine.

After we left the shipyard and headed back into downtown Bangkok and the Royal Orchid Hotel, Thaitek's Dr Pryor called Rivers on my mobile advising him he had received a message from the owner and chairman of the board of Sasco, Khun Mechi. He explained that Khun Mechi had implied that he intended meeting with government officials with intentions of exposing Eastern regarding the illegal under the table commission payments made by their agent Thaitek, also the mishandling of the government awarded contract for the procurement of the three by thirty-inch Dredges.

The following day Rivers and I met with the multi-millionaire owner of RomaThai Marine shipyard, a Thai-born Chinese in his late seventies. Dr Lee was a medical doctor by profession. He told us he enjoyed construction and shipbuilding much more than he did cutting into people, he added that these days his greatest pleasure was growing grapes and turning them into wine, he had several vineyards in the North East of Thailand near the Lao border. He told us of his lifetime friend from Rome, Italy and how together, more than forty years ago, they had formed a construction company and later ventured into shipbuilding. They had christened their company 'RomaThai' giving both equal representations in the title.

Also because of RomaThai's contribution to Thailand, theirs was the only construction and shipbuilding company in the country to be presented, by the King of Thailand, with the Royal emblem 'The Garuda Bird', which was proudly displayed on the façade of his new multi-storied office building in the heart of the business center in Bangkok.

In Thai mythology the Garuda Bird is known as the king of birds, it is an ancient and enduring symbol that serves as the royal insignia and is also the official seal of the Thai government. The characteristics of the Garuda are very much like an eagle and it is typically shown with the bill and wings of a bird, the body and limbs of a man with a white face, a green coloured body and red mouth. Bronze Garuda's adorn royal sedans and embellish the throne; the most familiar image of the Garuda Bird shows him holding a serpent in each taloned hand. It is also notable that the Garuda is symbolised in the Thai philosophy of wisdom.

Dr Lee then told us to clear all of the current problems

between Eastern and Sasco and he could guarantee Government Authority Approval within two weeks for the right to build the three Dredges in his shipyard, he then gave Rivers and myself two bottles of wine each from his vineyards and we departed.

I received a telephone call from Thaitek's Dr Pryor asking me if I could call and make an appointment to visit yet another Bangkok shipyard called 'Malvan Marine'. He told me the owners were good friends of his but under the current circumstances; he felt he couldn't approach them himself as he had been the prime mover in bringing Sasco and Eastern together. I called and made arrangements for Rivers and myself to visit the following day. After a guided tour of the shipyard conducted by Malvan Marine personnel, we discussed the Dredger project with the yards senior partner Khun Monchi, another Thai-born Chinese.

He told Rivers and I that he had very high political connections within the Thai government as well as the Ports and Rivers Authority. He continued that his sources had informed him that the Director General would, within the coming week, forward a letter to Eastern Dredging Co. advising them that as the schedule to build the Dredges had begun and no Thai shipyard approval had been granted, Eastern should proceed as per the Ports and Rivers Authority/Eastern contract and build in the United States. According to Monchi, this would clear the air and sever any agreement with Sasco, let the dust settle for two or three weeks, he said, then bring the project back to Thailand and Malvan Marine Shipyard. Senior partner Monchi continued that Sasco's MD Chang was bad mouthing Eastern Dredging Co. all over Bangkok. He had telephoned each and every shipyard in Thailand, which was only a half dozen or so that could handle a project of this magnitude, advising them not to bid quote the Eastern project.

We had lunch with the Malvan Marine people, then left to meet again with Dr Lee at RomaThai Marine. He told us he had just come from a business lunch with Director General Allrot who had explained the Sasco/Eastern situation and had advised the good doctor to be very careful of any arrangement with Eastern's owner Brown as he was perceived to be a totally untrustworthy businessman, an understatement I thought.

Dr Lee told us that if his shipyard signed a contract with Eastern and commenced to build the Dredges, Sasco could and would file a 'Stop Work' injunction on the project, which could be in court up to five years. In Thailand all a lawyer has to do is call in sick and a postponement of trial is no problem. Court delays can go on forever, and he quoted a German Dredge company that had been in litigation in Bangkok for the past seven years disputing the capability of Dredge engines.

His final remarks were that RomaThai's bid price would stand, but until Eastern clears everything with Sasco, he would not pursue the project any further. We thanked him and left. I was having a hard time believing all the shit that was happening, I was amazed that people actually conducted business in this manner, these Eastern folk were a bunch of crazy bastards.

Rivers told me on the way back to his hotel not to let anyone at Thaitek learn of the price quoted by RomaThai Marine, tomorrow we were to obtain a price from Malvan Marine shipyard, Rivers thoughts were that as Thaitek were buddies with the Malvan Marine owners they would inform Malvan Marine and the result would be price manipulation.

The following morning I met with Rivers at his hotel for breakfast and we discussed the project developments, seemed he didn't have much idea where it was headed and decided it was time to call Baltimore. We went to his room and he called Brown at his home explaining to him the situation to date, with emphasis on the RomaThai Marine advice and that he would be meeting with both the Ports and Rivers Authority and Malvan Marine shipyard later in the day. Brown's reaction was a re-negotiation of price with Sasco, he advised Rivers to contact Sasco's MD Chang and set up a meeting. After he hung up the telephone, Rivers became agitated with Brown's instructions and told me he would think about it for a couple of hours before he made his decision as to whether or not he would make contact with Chang. I thought it was the smartest piece of advice I had ever known Brown to give.

Later in the day, we met unofficially with several members of the inspection committee. Rivers was given an official letter by vice-chairman Piboon that had been signed by Director General Allrot advising Eastern to settle their problems with the Sasco shipyard and commence building the Dredges; this was obviously not the letter that Malvan Marine's senior partner Monchi had referred to the previous day.

After lunch, Rivers sent a facsimile to Sasco requesting they contact him for a meeting to discuss the Dredger project. We then left his hotel to visit Malvan Marine shipyard to answer any questions they may have regarding the blueprint drawings we had left with them the day before and to receive their bid price.

Rivers suggested to them during the discussions that he considered a fair price for the construction of the Dredges to be $5.5million. The Malvan Marine people discussed this price in rapid Thai, the little Thai that I could pick up was that their price was $5.9 million, they told Rivers they were close to his suggested price but needed another twenty–four hours to count their beans and would confirm a price the following day.

As we drove back to Rivers' hotel, I explained what I figured the price was they had mentioned, he once again told me how he didn't want the Thaitek agency involved in the negotiations as he did not trust them after his experiences with Eastern's agent in Indonesia. Apparently, the agent that Eastern had engaged for assistance with the Indonesian government and military chiefs had demanded one and a half million dollars for under the table commissions. Twenty-four hours after the money was transferred to the agent's account in Jakarta, the agent and the money disappeared, never to be seen again. Rivers believed Thaitek's only concern regarding Eastern was how many dollars they could extract from Brown.

Breakfast again with Rivers, who told me of a further conversation with Brown regarding utilising the Sasco shipyard, but Rivers explained, as he had not received any response from his facsimile requesting a meeting, he had persuaded Brown to wait for the Malvan Marine price.

I was beginning to become concerned with all the stupid shit these dickheads from Eastern were pulling; it was quite obvious they had no concept regarding the psyche of the people they were fucking with. To add fuel to my concerns was an article in the *'Bangkok Post'* newspaper regarding a daylight assassination that had just occurred in the sugar industry in the central Thai province of Nakon Sawan.

Owing to Thailand's economic woes, three sugar mills controlled by one family became involved in the ugly incident during a debt-restructuring program. A foreign chartered accountant, whose team of professionals was appointed by a Thai bankruptcy court to work on a debt-restructuring program for the three sugar mills, was shot to death as he travelled to work in a van. The shooting occurred as the vehicle slowed at a bend in the road about five hundred meters from one of the mills. An inspection of the murder scene revealed that seven of the eight bullets fired from the 11mm handgun had hit the accountant at fatal points, while four Thais also travelling in the van were unhurt. This evidence stunned the police and gave an idea of the skill of the gunman who at the time of the shooting was riding passenger on a black unmarked motorcycle.

After breakfast we were picked up by a company I had contacted to build the three Floating Pipelines. We were driven in a Mercedes-Benz to their plant for an inspection tour and later taken for lunch in one of the most expensive Chinese restaurants in Bangkok, which served such delicacies as Fish Guts Soup and Shark Fins. This was Asian food I could not eat, even the smell made me feel like throwing up.

After lunch, we were driven back to the Royal Orchid where a telephone message was waiting for Rivers requesting he call Thaitek. After the call, he told me that Malvan Marine shipyard had a price and wanted us to go visit with them.

We spent an hour with the Malvan Marine people, the senior partner, Monchi, gave us a history lesson of how to obtain the required responses from civil servants and government officials in Thailand, the bottom line was under the table commissions, and that was, according to Monchi, how Malvan Marine had reached their price. Rivers thanked them for their time and told them Eastern would consider their offer and would contact them with a decision within a week.

During the thirty-kilometre drive through the Bangkok freeway traffic system back to the hotel, Rivers said to me, 'See I told you those fucken bandits at Thaitek are playing money games.'

The Malvan Marine price quoted was $12 million, a big increase from the US $5.9 million the previous day. Rivers figured there was at least one million dollars for Thaitek in the price, 'Call it a finder's fee if you want,' he said, 'but those pricks are going to get their share you can bet on that.'

That evening I drove Rivers, via the express tollway, to Bangkok's Don Muang International airport for his flight back to the USA, before leaving he told me Brown would be in Bangkok the following week, I guessed decision time was drawing closer.

The expressways, bridges and fly-overs that form the interconnecting artery system of Bangkok are a symbol of progress in a developing country, however for some individuals they merely provide shelter that they call home. The money that was spent building these symbols of progress was the magnet that lured the poor, uneducated rural people to the city for work during the construction. When the building phase ended and unemployment soared due to the economic meltdown, they ended up living beneath them. It's estimated that more than eight hundred families live under approximately seventy bridges in Bangkok. One resident, a woman in her thirties, described how she came with her father as an eight-year-old girl and has been living under a bridge near the Don Muang International airport for twenty-odd years. She tells how her father had neither land nor money and decided to move to the city for construction work. By the time she was fifteen she was married and a mother.

CHAPTER 7

BROWN ARRIVED IN BANGKOK and requested that Dr Pryor from Thaitek and myself meet with him at his hotel. He advised us that before he left Baltimore, he had Rivers facsimile a message to Sasco that his intentions were to terminate the Eastern/Sasco agreement. After the discussion, Brown and Pryor went to a local law firm that Pryor did business with on Silom Road to have a formal letter of injunction drawn up. Within hours, the response from Sasco was received at Thaitek and it was hostile, Thaitek's Khun Terdsak telephoned me and advised me to stay clear of the Sasco shipyard, according to Terdsak they were ready to kill.

The following morning, a breakfast meeting was held with Brown, Thaitek and the Malvan Marine shipyard owners. During the meeting, the Malvan Marine people stated they could only build the three Dredges, no Tender Boats or Floating Pipeline and because of the reduction in work, they would reduce their price from $12 million to $9.6 million, Brown snapped it up instantly.

That afternoon the Thaitek agency received a telephone

call from vice-chairman Piboon of the Inspection committee. It was obvious the deal was old news, as Piboon informed Thaitek that the committee members and the Director General were immensely annoyed with Eastern and unofficially told Thaitek that if the Dredgers were not built in the Sasco shipyard then there was no way that the Dredges would be built in Thailand.

That evening a further meeting with Malvan Marine people to clarify contractual issues concluded at one am, to the satisfaction of all parties. Brown and I walked through the contract by speakerphone with Smitty, Rivers and the weekend warrior Johnson in Baltimore.

It was agreed they would email to me the corrected version before the close of their business day (our Bangkok morning), whereupon the concerned parties would meet again for a breakfast meeting and the official signing. Brown told his people in Baltimore that if he had to use the United States Embassy to achieve his goal, he would.

The following morning I printed off the 28-page contract and delivered it to the breakfast meeting at the Royal Orchid Hotel, where both Malvan Marine representatives and Brown signed. However before any construction could begin the Inspection committee had to inspect and approve the Malvan Marine shipyard, which, according to Malvan Marine's senior partner, Monchi, was not going to be a problem and he told Brown his yard would be approved within two weeks.

That afternoon there was a message left on my telephone answering machine from an individual who identified himself as a Sasco employee, stating he was inquiring after my health, now I knew it was time to check the rear-view mirrors for that black unmarked motorcycle.

After the contract signing, Brown returned to Baltimore and for the next couple of weeks Malvan Marine shipyard owners lobbied their contacts within the Ports and Rivers Authority and the Ministry of Shipping and Commerce of the Government of Thailand.

This ministry was headed by Minister Annop, who was supported by two Deputy Ministers—Sanit and Somboon. The Ports and Rivers Authority was under the control of Deputy Minister Sanit.

Towards the end of the second week after Brown's departure, Thaitek's Dr Pryor contacted me and advised that Sasco had requested a meeting with Eastern on the premise of lowering their $19 million price tag; I informed both Smitty and Rivers. The following day I received information that Smitty would be arriving in Bangkok in a couple of days for negotiations with Sasco.

I telephoned Smitty and warned him to be careful on his arrival at Bangkok's Don Muang International airport. A recent article in the 'Bangkok Post' had reported that police investigators were looking for several foreigners believed to have collaborated with an arrested Egyptian and his Thai wife in the murder of six tourists who had been picked up shortly after passing through the airports' international arrivals. The suspects were believed to have lured the visiting tourists, all European, into an unlicensed taxi before robbing, killing and then dumping their naked victim's bodies in various Bangkok suburbs. Airport security insisted there was not much they could do to stop the criminals prowling the airport, as it was impossible to keep the con men and crooks out of a public place. One official also stated that well-dressed crooks in suits are the worst as tourists are fooled by smart appearances. 'These people are immaculately dressed, are well-educated and they know how to talk and get what they want,' he stated.

Smitty arrived and told me that the following day Eastern's

purchasing agent and engineering manager draftsman Ted would be arriving in Bangkok from Seoul, South Korea where they had been visiting Korean Foundries regarding possible work for Eastern. He also informed me that at the end of the current month, he would no longer be working for Eastern because of the backstabbing and bullshit created by the weekend warrior Johnson and Ted. He had grown tired of the daily arguments, which on several occasions had come close to physical confrontation. He figured it just wasn't worth it any longer and had secured a position with a large international oil company, where he would head up their offshore division. This was a surprise and it was also sad that Smitty, in my opinion, was the only individual in the Eastern organisation that had his shit together when it came to the Dredger contract, plus he was highly respected by the Thais for his knowledge and attitude.

The project manager Rivers was an okay guy but he was a salesman, not an engineer, and therefore could not give me or the Inspection Committee the technical support required for the project, also like the majority of salesmen, he had a tendency to exaggerate.

After their arrival the following day, I drove the purchasing agent and draftsman Ted to the Joint Venture Shipyard - Prakarn, the steel plate had arrived on site and the keel laying of the twenty-inch Dredger had begun.

Smitty had arranged a two o'clock meeting at the Royal Orchid hotel with Sasco management and I arrived back at the hotel in time to join the meeting.

Both draftsman Ted and the purchasing agent made excuses about needing to clean up and headed for their rooms. Ted was scared shitless—he had heard about the Sasco telephone call requesting information regarding my health plus the black unmarked motorcycle stories.

I joined Smitty and was informed that MD Chang had been temporarily relieved of duty owing to stress and his assistant Khun Suwat was now running the show for Sasco. As I sat down, assistant Suwat was explaining to Smitty that Eastern's agent Thaitek was up to no good, and was double-dealing. Also, Thaitek had informed Sasco that I had been delivering thirty-inch Dredger blueprint drawings to every shipyard in the Bangkok area. I spoke up, even though Smitty tried to hush me, and told Suwat that I worked for Eastern and therefore I followed instructions from Eastern and if that meant delivering blueprint drawings to various shipyards then that is what I did. But I was thinking what a bunch of back-stabbing Motherfuckers Thaitek turned out to be.

Assistant Suwat accepted my explanation and then told Smitty and myself that Sasco would not alter their price or scope of work. He had concrete information from inside the Thai government ministry responsible for the Ports and Rivers Authority, that if the Dredges were not built in his yard then there was absolutely no way the Dredges would be built in Thailand.

After the Sasco meeting, Eastern personnel and the Inspection committee met and discussed the twenty-inch Dredger project, which was progressing on schedule. The committee advised Eastern to mend the bridges with Sasco or make the decision to build the thirty-inch Dredges in the United States as the contract had been in effect for six months and two milestone dates—shipment of main engines and keel lay—had come and gone and time was of the essence.

Smitty gave each committee member a small gift he had carried with him from Baltimore and said his goodbyes, the committee members said they were saddened to see him go, but wished him well. That evening they took him to several entertainment venues in Bangkok for an evening of sex, drugs and karaoke. After his return to Baltimore, he telephoned me several days before his departure from Eastern Dredging Co. to say farewell, his only comment regarding his final evening in Bangkok was, 'Amazing Thailand.'

Like many countries throughout the world, Thailand has a problem involving narcotics. The supply of amphetamine pills, known locally as, 'Ya Ba', pour across the northern Thai–Burma border. Burma, with its military dictatorship, is in collusion with the drug warlords of the Golden Triangle who own the Ya Ba factories along the border. One of the world's largest armed narcotic trafficking gangs—the Burma based United WA State Army, whose stronghold is on the Burmese–Chinese border, has in the past decade established a presence on the Thai–Burma border across from the northern Thai province of Chang-Mai. In a recent clash along the border, Thai soldiers engaged in a shoot-out with United WA State Army soldiers, killing several and recovering over five million Ya Ba pills with a street value of more than one hundred million Baht, AK-47 assault rifles and grenade launchers, discarded by the fleeing WA Army soldiers.

CHAPTER 8

THE JOINT VENTURE SHIPYARD - Prakarn had, within several months, completed the building of the keel and was in the process of fabricating the hull. I had met with the twenty-inch Inspection committee chairman, Capt. Chitepong who had approved all blueprint drawings and passed them on to me for shipyard delivery.

He was also proving to be a helpful and likeable individual. He had one peculiarity that I couldn't help notice; every time I was in his presence, he was wearing a different expensive genuine Rolex wristwatch.

I had also met with a company regarding the construction of the three Floating Pipelines. After several hours of discussion and viewing the blueprint drawings, the two Thai representatives asked me how much commission I would require, I was astounded at how open and nonchalant they were.

When I hesitated with a response they told me, don't worry about it, we just add it on top of our price and pay it into your bank account—it's standard practice in Thailand. I told them

I would have to think about it, which they accepted, then rolled up the drawings. We said our goodbyes with them telling me they should have a bid quote price in several weeks.

The thirty-inch project was becoming chaotic, according to Rivers, the weekend warrior's engineering department was two months behind schedule and he was looking for a company in the United States to help pull him out of the engineering shit. Malvan Marine shipyard had not received Ports and River Authority approval. Brown was flip-flopping about shipyards, asking could I contact RomaThai Marine shipyard and maybe bring them back into the picture. He was again considering a new offer to Sasco, requesting me to telephone assistant Suwat and ask for a 1.1 million price reduction. I did, Suwat responded with the answer, 'Speak with MD Chang.' whose response was a loud and very distinctive, 'No.' I wasn't sure if he had been stress relieved or not.

Malvan Marine informed Eastern Dredging Co. and myself, that if the project was to remain in Thailand, they would require one million dollars as an under the table commission for the Shipping and Commerce Deputy Minister, whom they had been lobbying. There would also have to be an overall price reduction of one million, refunded to the Ports and Rivers Authority. I received a telephone call from Thaitek's Dr Pryor, who ranted about Brown not paying his bills, about not receiving his $50,000 per month service fee and still no reimbursement for his supposed under the table commission payments.

He added that he was considering withdrawing his services, also advising that if the project was to remain in Thailand, the inspection committee would have to approve the Malvan Marine shipyard. For this service he told me, the committee members were requesting a million dollars, totalled up, that would mean a three million dollar payout for Brown.

Well Thaitek wasn't the only party having problems receiving payment from Eastern. On a monthly basis, I would have to continuously request my salary, receiving it ten to fourteen days late. On one occasion, I complained to Rivers that if it wasn't in my bank account within forty–eight hours I would sell both the laptop computer and the Isuzu pick-up truck as compensation.

Early April, Rivers and Brown arrived in Bangkok with the intention of confirming a Thai shipyard. Sasco's final offer was a price reduction of three hundred thousand dollars off the contract price; this to be refunded to the Ports and Rivers Authority and paid by Eastern, plus the Dredges to be built in the Sasco yard. This deal they said was fully accepted by Director General Allrot, also Sasco informed Eastern once again that their agent, Thaitek, had no integrity.

Brown dismissed the offer and had Thaitek arrange a meeting with Deputy Minister Sanit so that he could present his proposal of utilising Malvan Marine shipyard and reimburse the Thai government half a million dollars off the contract price.

The Deputy Minister told Brown to get serious, he explained that if he went to parliament and explained to his government colleagues that Eastern would deduct a half million dollars—a miniscule amount in his mind—and utilise a different shipyard as previously contractually stated, he would be questioned as to how much he had accepted as an under the table commission. 'No,' he told Brown, 'you have a choice, you either build at the Sasco yard in Thailand or you build in the United States as your contract dictates.'

According to Rivers, during the meeting with the Deputy Minister, Brown with his usual sarcastic tongue alienated himself. When it came to business sense and dealing with the Thais, Brown had his head up his ass.

There were several other factors against Brown—during the US/Vietnam conflict of the 1960s, the now-Deputy Minister had attended University in the US city of New Orleans, on one particular occasion he had entered a New Orleans restaurant but was refused service and ordered to leave by the redneck owner with the words, 'We don't serve Gooks in here.' Another strike against Brown was that the owner of Sasco, Khun Mechi, was an adviser to Deputy Minister Sanit and a personal friend. Brown was fucked, he preached about how he would utilise his connections in Washington DC and the US Embassy in Bangkok to obtain his goal. This rhetoric ran like water off a duck's back.

The following morning after the Deputy Ministers' meeting, I along with Rivers and Brown had a breakfast meeting with the Malvan Marine's senior partner Khun Monchai, who told Brown he was getting too much heat from his countrymen and withdrew his shipyard, reiterating that Brown should go build the Dredges in the United States.

Thaitek's Dr Pryor showed up at the hotel and advised Brown that the Ports and Rivers Authority was now under instruction to send an Inspection party to Baltimore to view Eastern Dredging Co.'s facilities. This was with intentions of beginning the process of termination of the contract with Eastern and have the project for the three Dredges re-bid, accepting only Thai shipyards as eligible bidders. Both parties—Eastern and Malvan Marine, declared their contract null and void. Dr Pryor was telling myself, Brown and Rivers that he had paid vice chairman Piboon, of the Inspection committee, one million Baht, as an under the table commission to convince the other committee members towards the Malvan Marine shipyard approval. I was beginning to recognise a pattern to Dr Pryor's method of extracting mega-bucks from Eastern. Each crisis that faced Brown (which I was beginning to wonder if Dr Pryor hadn't orchestrated) required money to solve. He would advise Brown that he could remedy the problem with under the table commissions, when nothing happened, he would convince Brown that he had been double-crossed by the bandit politicians and inspection committee members. Each time Brown fell for it, and Dr Pryor was smiling all the way to his Singapore bank, well it was no use my worrying about the things I had no control over.

The following afternoon Rivers and Brown left for the US, Brown a defeated fool with his tail between his legs and Rivers with his ubiquitous loyalty, who couldn't see the forest for the trees. I could not bring myself to have sympathy for these guys; I had warned them when I was in Baltimore not to hoodwink the Thais when doing business with them. The Thais are a unique race of people.

Several days after his return, Rivers telephoned from Baltimore and told me he was in the process of signing a contract with a shipyard in New Orleans, for the construction of the three thirty-inch Dredgers.

I had a meeting with the Rolex-watch-and-diamond-ring-wearing committee and explained to them the information Rivers had relayed to me regarding the US Shipyard. They requested a letter of invitation from Eastern inviting two full-time inspectors to be stationed in New Orleans, and four committee members to visit Baltimore and the shipyard location for approval purpose. At the conclusion of the meeting, I invited all the committee members to wine and dine. They didn't require any persuasion, telling me the location they desired for an evening of profit and pleasure would be an establishment called 'The Plaza'.

'The Plaza' is a high-rise building of twenty floors; the first three floors are for parking the BMWs and Mercedes-Benz. The fourth floor is a combination of several bars and restaurants occupying two-thirds of the floor; the remaining floor space is a brightly illuminated glass-enclosed room filled with young Thai pooyings, (females), in their late teens and early twenties, each wearing an evening-type gown. The ladies are seated in a semi-circle on a carpet-covered terraced arrangement; attached to their gowns, in the vicinity of their left breast is a round white plastic badge bearing a black number.

Several Thai men dressed in ill-fitting cheap suits wander among the male patrons asking, 'Which number you like?' If wished, you could also sit in the bars or restaurants and look at one of the many television sets tuned to the glass-enclosed room panning the seated girls. If you desired a particular female, all you had to do was indicate to a waiter you had made your choice and an ill-fitting suit would get the order and the lady of your choice would join you at your table.

The committee arranged for a private room on the sixteenth floor, which was in fact a large condominium containing five bedrooms, a dining room with seating for a dozen guests and a television set for karaoke and viewing the selection of females in their glass room. Situated adjacent to the dining area was a large bubbling hot tub. After we were seated, the alcohol, Thai food and Thai pooyings appeared.

Piboon was seated beside me; within seconds, his arm was around a young beauty and he asked me what was my 'Spec'. I said, 'Spec?'

'Yes,' he said, 'big tits, little tits, black skin, brown skin, white skin, fat, skinny, tall, short whatever is your 'specification'—it's here.' Khun Preecha from Thaitek and Capt. Chitepong were seated across the table from me, they were discussing the girls by their number, and judging by their conversation this was not their first visit. Preecha was saying, 'Number eleven gives good service and smokes Ganja, number twenty–two, her service is no good, she no smoke kuay.' (perform oral sex—kuay is the Thai slang for penis).

It was a matter-of-fact conversation, Thai style. Sexist as it seemed, this was a place of business and sexual performance by the seller, in an over-populated industry, was important to the buyer—the evening cost Eastern several thousand dollars.

CHAPTER 9

I WAS VISITING THAITEK'S OFFICE at least three to four times a week for the purpose of documentation submittals to comply with the bureaucracy of the Ports and Rivers Authority. All submittals connected with the twenty-inch project had to be in the Thai language; Thaitek's Preecha was utilised as translator. Communications for the thirty-inch project were English, which all members of the inspection committee were fluent in, several having attended universities in the United States. Vice Chairman Piboon had attained his degree in Naval Architecture at the Ann Arbor University in the state of Michigan.

Each time I was in Thaitek's office, Dr Pryor and his cohorts would lambaste Piboon as the worst type of Thai that existed. He was a crook, a liar, always asking for money, and never assisting the Eastern project, plus he was a spy for the Sasco shipyard.

Seems they couldn't make enough derogatory remarks about the guy. After weeks of listening to these prolonged speeches of abuse, I asked Dr Pryor why he didn't do like so many others do in Thailand and hire a couple of guys on a black unmarked motorcycle and eliminate the problem. 'Oh no, we are not people like that,' he said, 'I will speak with the Director General and have Piboon removed from the inspection committee.'

'Good luck,' I replied, but I had my doubts—seemed all that Dr Pryor was any good at was extracting cash from Eastern's assbag Brown.

Eastern forwarded the letters of invitation for the US visit to the inspection committee and the two full time inspectors. According to the contract, Eastern was liable for all Ports and Rivers Authority representatives to travel first class, and receive full accommodation and living expenses; Eastern was also contractually obligated for a per diem payment to the full time inspectors of $265 while on site in the United States. I was approached by Thaitek's Terdsak and told that Vice Chairman Piboon wished to speak to me regarding the inspector's $265 per day payment. Piboon told me that he and Capt. Chitepong had discussed the per diem payment and figured it was too much for the inspectors to be receiving while they were in the US. He figured that he and Chitepong should hold $100 of the daily payment for the inspectors and give it to them on their return to Thailand.

I figured it was bullshit, these guys intended putting the cash in their ass national, but it wasn't my business and I relayed the message to Brown and Rivers whose only comment was, 'Looks like the Inspectors are buying their job. Eastern will pay the full amount to the Inspectors, what they do with it is up to them.'

The inspectors subserviently made the payment of the $100 per day and accepted the situation without question.

Thailand is an extremely sophisticated society; wealth, education, ethnic background; skin colour and employment-position dominate. Skin colour in Thailand is an immensely important issue. Thais are continuously bombarded by television commercials and advertisements before the main feature at movie theatres for cosmetic skin-whitening products and they are on every Thai Pooying's shopping list. White talcum powder is also utilised and rubbed into the facial skin to make it appear whiter. Thais, both male and female, cover themselves from head to foot when working outdoors to prevent any sun contact and skin tanning. A light skin coloured Pooying is highly prized among Thai males.

The inspectors were lower on the Totem Pole than either Piboon or Chitepong, and career-wise, it was not advisable to rock the boat. It was Thai style, for the inspectors to have accommodation and food supplied by Eastern plus the remaining $165 per day, was a good deal, and certainly a great supplement to the thirty to thirty–five hundred Baht per month salary they received from the government department they worked for.

The trip to the United States was organised for departure mid year, I would also join the entourage. A keel lay ceremony for the thirty-inch Dredgers would be held in the New Orleans shipyard and hopefully the committee would approve and sign-off, allowing Eastern to invoice for the keel lay milestone payment of 15 percent, which amounted to $7.5 million. There was one hitch, according to Thaitek's Dr Pryor—Director General Allrot of the Ports and Rivers Authority required an under the table commission of $300,000. I relayed the information to Brown; his reaction was, when he received his money he would then wire transfer the cash to Dr Pryor's Singapore account for payment to the Director General.

I discussed the visit to the US by the inspection committee with both Rivers and Brown, and reminded them of what the visitors would expect. Relating to the social structure of

Thailand and the government position that these guys held, and considering they wore Rolex watches and diamond rings, drove BMWs and Mercedes-Benz—they would be expecting VIP treatment, which meant they would not like handling their own luggage. They would expect Limousine service to and from airports, and they would require accommodation in five-star hotels. Both Rivers and Brown said they understood and would arrange everything. The itinerary of the trip was for three days in Baltimore, three days in New Orleans, one night and a full day in Los Angeles where the chairman of the committee had asked for a golf game to be arranged for himself and whoever wished to join him, and then return to Bangkok. Thaitek's Khun Preecha would also be joining the group.

After twenty–three hours of travelling non-stop, we arrived at Baltimore Washington International airport at 8.00 am. Rivers was there to meet and greet, telling me that he had his wife's minivan to transport us to the hotel, I reminded him about the Limo we had discussed, his response was, Brown figured the minivan would suffice. We collected the luggage, Rivers and I assisting the committee as much as our pride would allow. We waited outside the airport while Rivers went to get the van. The clean, crisp Baltimore morning air was a welcome extreme after the hot humid polluted air of Bangkok. Fifteen minutes later, Rivers showed up on foot and explained his key would not open the van door, which had him confused as it had worked earlier. He organised two old beat-up Chevrolet taxis to transport everyone to a hotel named the 'Red Roof'. The cab I found myself in was being driven by an old coot who obviously was not happy about the five-minute fare and amount of luggage his cab was carrying. Listening to his bullshit it was becoming hard to contain myself, I was jet-lagged, there was no limo, no minivan and now a cantankerous old assbag taxi driver. The fare cost $12; I borrowed $20 from Rivers, as I had no US currency, and handed it to the taxi driver telling him to go learn some manners, he called me an asshole and drove off.

Rivers, along with the committee chairman and several of the members had arrived at the hotel ahead of me. Thaitek's Khun Preecha came to me and said the chairman and his crew were not happy with the hotel, as I looked at the building it was not hard to figure out why. It was not a hotel, but a motel, and a Red Roofed Rat-Hole at that. I spoke with Rivers and told him the committee was pissed off big time—no limo, no van, vintage taxis and now a Rat Hole that didn't even have a restaurant. I continued, you want these guys on your side, don't forget they are the client and they are here to approve Eastern, its facilities, the shipyard and the keel lay, plus confirm the Eastern/Ports and Rivers Authority contract.

I was on a jet-lagged roll so I continued, 'I told both you and Brown these guys expected VIP treatment for Christ sake, now you had better get on the telephone and get a five star hotel before they return to the airport and haul-ass back to Bangkok!'

Rivers blamed Brown for hotel choice; however, he arranged for an upgrade a kilometre or so down the road called the 'Double Tree'. We had to convince the committee that we had only come to the Red Roof Rat Hole to rest until the Double Tree had cleaned the rooms, which had now happened and we could proceed in two minivans that Eastern had arranged.

The 'Double Tree' had an excellent restaurant where we ate a 10.00 am breakfast. The committee figured Eastern had attempted to pull a 'Cheap Charlie' deal, and didn't believe the story about the rooms being cleaned. They seemed a little cheered up after eating, and it was decided we would rest and meet to discuss the working itinerary for the next week at

3.00 pm. After the meeting, Rivers arranged for one of the
Eastern salesmen to take the committee chairman to a local
sports store and buy him a set of golf clubs for his game in
Los Angeles. The chairman would not go unless accompanied
by committee members Piboon and Chitepong.

He got his set of clubs—which cost Rivers $2,000—
while at the sports store, the salesman offered to purchase
a pro golfer's T-shirt for Piboon and Chitepong, which they
declined—more insults.

Things were not going well, I could not believe how naïve
these Eastern personnel were, after all, they claimed to be an
internationally operating company with projects in Egypt,
Vietnam and Indonesia, yet here they were treating a client
country's government representatives, who were travelling
on diplomatic passports, with contempt.

The three days in Baltimore were spent inspecting Eastern's facilities, listening to the weekend warrior lecture on
the Dredger engineering progress and purchasing department explaining their schedule, at night Eastern wined and
dined the committee and everyone seemed to be harmonising.
The more time I spent around Capt. Chitepong, the more I
liked the guy; he always had a quick-witted response to most
people's comments.

Before I left Thailand, I had visited one of the numerous goldsmith stores in the Chinatown area of Bangkok
and selected an exquisite large linked, twenty–four carat,
sixty-gram gold chain as requested by the vice president of
Eastern's human resources department, Ms Candy Lawford, at
a cost of $750. When I handed it to her, the first comment
was, 'Oh I don't like the colour, it looks like brass.' The gold
she wore was the dull yellow ten-carat type—Asian gold has
a brilliant gold sheen.

I listened to her negative bullshit for several minutes and

then told her, 'Don't worry about it, I can return it.' She immediately handed it back to me and I left her office thinking, what a fucken douche-bag bitch, she hadn't even thanked me for the effort of buying the fucken chain, that would be the last favour I'd do for that slut—I was pissed off!

We arrived in downtown New Orleans around noon on our fourth day and were checked into the now-familiar hotel chain, the 'Double Tree'. Vice chairman Piboon wanted to visit the shipyard immediately but Rivers told him, no, he would stick to the schedule and visit the following day as arranged. Piboon's response was, maybe the committee wouldn't go the following day.

One of the committee members, Khun Pax, a quiet individual who never spoke much but who was very close to both Piboon and Chitepong, took me aside and asked me where I thought the Dredgers were going to be built. I told him New Orleans, and asked him where *he* thought they would be built. He responded, 'Thailand, at the Sasco shipyard.' I was astonished at this statement and relayed it to Rivers who was equally confused.

The first night in New Orleans, a formal dinner had been arranged at one of the most famous restaurants in the city's French Quarter, 'Antoine's'. It was attended by the committee members; a management team from the shipyard contracted to build the Dredgers, Rivers and myself. Brown was flying down from Baltimore that afternoon and told Rivers he would meet with the dinner party at the restaurant no later than 7.30 pm.

We arrived at 'Antoine's' as scheduled, introductions were initiated but there was a feeling of anxiety, the Americans, including Rivers, hung together as did the Thais, and me—I just stood there like a fucking dickhead, not really knowing which group to join. By 8.00 pm Brown had not shown, twenty minutes later, still no Brown, both Piboon and Chitepong sidled up to me and said they were considering leaving, up to this moment we had been standing in the host lounge sipping drinks while waiting to be seated, which was stalled because of Brown's late arrival.

Finally, at 8.30 pm, Piboon and Chitepong, after further consultations with their chairman, told me they were leaving. When I asked why, they told me that they had not been formally advised as to whom would be in attendance, there was no Brown, and from their perspective, the committee chairman had been insulted.

Realising they were determined to leave; I asked if they wanted me to accompany them. They said no thanks, its no problem, we will just wander around the French Quarter and will see you at breakfast tomorrow and away the four committee members and two inspectors went.

The shipyard management team were totally confused, I told Rivers the reason for the walkout but he was at a loss for words. Brown, the owner and president of Eastern had done it again; arriving at 9.00 pm. We were then seated in a private room. He asked why the Thais had left, jokingly the shipyard people asked him if he still had a contract to build the Dredges.

After the dinner at 'Antoine's', I walked the half dozen blocks back to the 'Double Tree' hotel with Rivers and Brown, Thaitek's Khun Preecha had not joined the dinner party saying he was sick, maybe his countrymen had told him of their walkout intentions. During the walk to the hotel Brown told me Sasco had started court proceedings against Eastern, but, according to Brown, they had about as much chance as a snowball in hell of achieving anything. When we reached the hotel, Brown telephoned Thaitek's Dr Pryor in Bangkok complaining about the Thais walking out on the dinner party, plus they had inferred they might not visit the shipyard the following day for the keel lay inspection.

Brown requested that Pryor contact Director General All-rot of the Ports and Rivers Authority to bring pressure on the committee members.

The following morning at 9.00 am utilising the two mini-vans that had been hired to bring us from the New Orleans airport to the hotel, everyone except Brown (who would follow later) departed for the shipyard. Pryor had returned Brown's telephone call and stated he had visited with the Director General and the committee would visit the ship-yard, however they were there to observe and it was their call whether or not to approve the keel lay.

The shipyard wasn't much to look at—a couple of office buildings and one steel fabrication shop. Separating the buildings from the Mississippi river was a ten-foot high levee, between the levee and the river's edge was a flat stretch of land of approximately one hundred yards wide, where, lined up in a row, were three sets of steel plates welded together, each set sitting on top of concrete blocks, each set representing a Dredger keel. This would be the second keel lay ceremony I would witness for the three Dredgers. The committee members were recording the facilities and Dredger keels on video and still photographs.

We had been at the shipyard about an hour and a half, when the committee members approached Rivers and said they were satisfied, they had seen enough and were ready to depart. They also asked why Brown wasn't present, Rivers told them Brown was on the way, but the traffic in New Orleans was causing his delay. He also told the committee that a Buddhist Monk was on the way to bless the keels and the local New Orleans newspaper—*The Times-Picayune*, would be doing an article and taking photographs of the event—the committee members showed no interest.

The Monk arrived and was escorted to the middle keel

where he commenced his blessing. The committee members were standing on top of the levee bank watching the proceedings, halfway through the blessing they all turned and walked away. At the completion of the blessing and newspaper photographs, Rivers paid the Monk $200 for his time and we all walked back up over the levee to the main office building and rejoined the waiting committee members. Brown had just arrived, late again; he requested a meeting with the committee chairman.

Both committee members Piboon and Chitepong joined the chairman. Brown immediately complained about the walk-out the previous evening, there was no apology regarding his absence at the keel lay blessing or his late arrival at the dinner party, he was just verbally hostile, a total dickhead. The chairman and his companion's listened, as polite Thai folk do, then excused themselves saying they needed to confer with the other committee members.

Twenty minutes later, the chairman and Piboon approached me and requested transportation back to the 'Double Tree' hotel, they also stated they could not approve the keel lay for milestone payment until they returned to Bangkok and had a meeting with their Director General.

Brown was furious, saying, 'To hell with them, there will be no golf game in Los Angeles!' Rivers was to travel to Los Angeles with the committee, act as chaperone and pay the bills until we departed for Bangkok. River's trip was cancelled; Brown had him travel back to Baltimore with him that afternoon, which would leave me alone with the Thais.

I told Brown to turn in the rented minivans; I would get the committee members to the New Orleans airport the following morning and for him not to worry. I organised the longest blackest limousine in New Orleans to transport us all to the airport the following morning. When the Thais saw the limo they commented, 'Now this is our style.' Of course it was, I had learned that, *and* I would send the bill to Eastern.

The New Orleans newspaper ran several photographs of the Monk blessing the Dredger keels along with the article headlined, *'Monk blesses Thai ships, $10 million deal has New Orleans shipyard busy.'* The article described the blessing ceremony, how it was in keeping with the Thai cultural tradition of blessing or dedicating the keel of a vessel and how the ritual was held for the visiting members of the Royal Thailand Ports and Rivers Authority. It was then explained that the shipyard was building the three Dredgers for Eastern Dredging Company of Baltimore for $10 million, and that Eastern had received a $50 million contract from the Thailand Ministry of Shipping and Commerce to build and outfit the Dredgers. It also reported that the shipyard had only been purchased five months earlier by the current owner Gemco Inc. and that the project breathed new life into the old shipyard and would generate one hundred and ten new jobs. The cat was out of the bag. The members of the inspection committee had been told Eastern owned the shipyard. Before they departed New Orleans, they purchased several copies of the latest edition of *The Times-Picayune*, which carried the article.

Before leaving Los Angeles, Rivers telephoned me, saying Brown was back negotiating with Sasco, he added that Thaitek's Dr Pryor had informed him that the committee vice chairman Piboon had been reporting on a daily basis to Sasco all events that occurred during the visit to the US. According to Rivers, it seemed Sasco had a whole lot more political power than Brown ever imagined, eventually Brown surrendered and agreed that Sasco would get the contract for the three Tender Boats and three Floating Pipelines plus $3 million—a contract worth \$8.2 million. It was obvious that Sasco, the Director General and Deputy Minister Sanit had united and given Brown an ultimatum, deal with Sasco for the three Tender Boats and Floating Pipelines and compensate them for their shipyard revamping prior to the Dredger project being pulled, or have his Ports and Rivers Authority contract terminated. Well, that meant I would not be picking up any easy money as suggested by Rivers a couple of months earlier.

CHAPTER 10

S EVERAL DAYS AFTER RETURNING from the US, I met for lunch with Capt. Chitepong, who told me Brown was number one on the 'most disliked persons list' at the Ports and Rivers Authority. He added that if Eastern wanted to play games, then so would the inspection committee and that would mean problems for Brown.

According to the Eastern/Ports and Rivers Authority contract, the location of Eastern's shipyard in the US was Baltimore, Maryland, not New Orleans, Louisiana. In fact, as exposed in the New Orleans newspaper article, Eastern did not possess a shipyard, the New Orleans yard was only contracted to build the Dredges, therefore, contractually, Eastern was between a rock and a hard place. The inspection committee was pushing to have the project returned to Thailand.

The following week I received a copy of a fax directed to Brown from Thaitek, which had originated at the Ports and Rivers Authority. It requested proof of shipyard ownership by Eastern of the project-designated shipyard.

The only way out for Eastern was to forward copies of all

contracts and lease arrangements with affidavits stating it was Eastern's standard practice that shipyard facilities were hired for hull construction, meanwhile all engineering and parts would come from Eastern's facilities or designated sub-contractors.

The Director General and his inspection committee forwarded all information to the Attorney General of Thailand requesting a written decision whether to accept or reject. Four weeks later Eastern received approval. Thaitek's Dr Pryor claimed he had paid an under the table commission amounting to $250,000 to several government ministers. However there was no way Eastern could verify whose ass national received the money, Brown dutifully wire transferred cash to Pryor's Singapore account.

Meanwhile, Rivers had telephoned me complaining about draftsman Ted and his interference with the project, telling me that Ted would be in Bangkok in a couple of weeks and asked if I could arrange to have him photographed in a sexually explicit situation, he didn't care if Ted's involvement was with male or female, just the younger the better. I laughed at this request, thinking the guy was joking but he was serious and he added that when Ted had travelled with him to visit the project in Indonesia he was a regular customer at Jakarta's houses of prostitution. Therefore, it shouldn't be a problem to entice him into a situation in one of Bangkok's Pat Pong or Nana Plaza sex establishments. He added he needed some dirt on Ted to keep him in check.

Rivers had always spoken of himself as a religious person, a born-again Christian who taught Sunday school, this was a contradiction, he must have figured Ted was way out of line, I told Rivers I would look into it.

There are traditions in Thailand that dictate strict adherence. Virginity is one of these traditions. As a young Thai female approaches marrying age, her mother usually arranges the marriage with another family she feels is in the best interest of all concerned, the marrying couple have very little to say about it. The groom's family provide a dowry with the proviso that the bride is a virgin and will be dutiful and faithful to her husband. Many of these marriages fail. The blame is always on the girl and her family, now no longer a virgin and having caused disgrace to the family, she is virtually worthless; adding to this disgrace the girl's family is expected to repay the dowry. Because of huge areas of poverty in Thailand, the lack of education due to the cost and no training programs, the majority of the girls coming from a failed marriage or the loss of virginity outside of marriage mean employment opportunities are extremely limited, amounting to mainly construction labour or the bars. The potential for the money to be made in the bars far exceeds the low labour wages, which entices them to the bright lights. Most of the girls feel the prime objective is to gain back the respect of their families and do so by sending their hard-earned cash home and in most cases the girls parents do not know she is selling her body. Many of these girls come from the poverty stricken areas and are in the business for one reason and that is to make money to support their family—a huge majority are the sole provider.

Another accepted tradition among married Thai men that often leads to failed marriages is the 'Mia Noi', which means second or minor wife but is in reality, a mistress. All of these reasons equate to a steady supply of bar girls. With this in mind, I knew there would be no problem of getting draftsman Ted in a compromising position if that was to be my intention.

The twenty-inch Dredge project at the Joint Venture Shipyard was progressing without a problem, every Saturday

I would spend five or six hours going over the construction with Captain Somboon as that was the only free time he had, owing to his naval duties. The shipyard owner Khun Savit was in hospital for the second time in several months for a partial removal of his small intestine, the doctors had told his wife if there was a recurrence then she would need to make funeral arrangements, but for now, the old guy was hanging in.

The Ports and Rivers Authority set up another committee for the administration of the Trade and Development Agency training grant of $400,000, of which Capt. Chitepong was elected chairman. Terdsak of the Thaitek agency told me he had met with Chitepong for discussions on how the training of personnel, trips to the US and distribution of the grant would be organised.

Terdsak told me Capt. Chitepong had requested $300,000 be utilised for the training program and the remaining $100,000 would go to himself and he would share it with the other three committee members.

This was just another under the table commission payment, a fucken rip-off of US taxpayer's money. Presumably, it would also assist Eastern regarding improved cooperation from the Inspection committee.

I relayed the information regarding the $100,000 to Brown and Rivers. Brown stated Dr Pryor had informed him of the situation; Rivers added, 'Those little brown rice eaters sure like Uncle Sam's hand-outs.'

Rivers also told me he would require me to move to New Orleans and assist with the thirty-inch Dredger project, I told him, 'No problem, but we would have to re-negotiate my contract.' He replied he would be back in Thailand in several weeks and we would discuss it.

CHAPTER 11

I SUBMITTED THIRTEEN BLUEPRINT DRAWINGS of the thirty-inch Dredgers to the Ports and Rivers Authority for client approval. The drawings submitted bore an official Eastern letterhead written in the Thai language stating they were for the twenty-inch project, though during the weekend I realised I had made a mistake. On Monday morning I visited the office of the chairman of the inspection committee for the twenty-inch Dredger project, Capt. Chitepong, and explained my dilemma, he was very helpful and immediately rounded them up, thus allowing me to re-submit under the correct project designation. Vice chairman Piboon of the thirty-inch project inspection committee was in Capt. Chitepong's office and offered to take the drawings and internally submit them without a re-submittal letter from Eastern. I accepted his offer, not knowing the ramifications this action would create in the months to come.

Brown was dragging his feet regarding his signing of the contract with Sasco. Daily, he was telephoning Thai-tek and asking where his keel lay milestone payment was.

The onsite Ports and Rivers Authority inspectors in New Orleans had reported to their superiors that the keels conformed to the contract and the shipyard was now legally viable. Thaitek's Dr Pryor was becoming agitated; he was receiving threatening telephone calls from Sasco, stating they would commence legal action regarding the Tender Boat and Pipeline contract.

Finally Dr Pryor informed Brown he had met with Director General Allrot and had been told that Sasco had paid $1 million as an under the table commission to Deputy Minister Sanit, of the Shipping and Commerce Ministry, who was the Director General's superior. Deputy Minister Sanit, as a favour to Sasco, instructed Director General Allrot not to make the keel lay payment, worth $7.5 million to Eastern, until Brown signed the Sasco/Eastern contract.

According to the Eastern/Ports and Rivers Authority contract, milestone payments would be made as named events occurred. There was to be six payments—1) down payment at completion of contract documentation $7.5 million; 2) shipment of main engines $7.5 million; 3) keel lay $7.5 million; 4) shipment of Dredge pump and gearbox $12.5 million; 5) shipment of vessels $10 million and finally, 6) acceptance by the inspection committee, $5 million.

Brown was running low on cash. He sent a derogatory letter to the inspection committee advising them that from his point of view, they were late with the keel lay milestone payment. Contractually, the committee had forty–five days to make the payment after invoice submittal with all required documentation. However, what Brown failed to understand was the listing of milestone payments in the Eastern/Ports and Rivers Authority contract and the ramifications of changing them for both the committee and Director General. The keel lay payment was listed and agreed to by both parties as third payment; Eastern had received only the first payment, which was the 'down payment at completion of contract documentation'. The second payment as listed was 'shipment of main engines'. To convince the committee to change the payment schedule was not an easy task.

The internal politics of the Ports and Rivers Authority dictated that the Director General and his committee follow the contract to the letter. If they were to deviate without just cause and ample documentation to support the deviation, they could jeopardise their careers. Internal audits of projects were conducted by high-ranking government Deputy Ministers and their staff. It was an extremely bureaucratic machine and no committee member or the Director General was going to ruin his career for Brown, especially when many had reportedly bought their positions. I had been told by Thaitek's Dr Pryor that the reigning Director General Allrot had paid $1.5 million for his office, and when his tenure was completed he would be promoted to Permanent Secretary of the Thai governments Shipping and Commerce Ministry.

Eastern never seemed to get the paperwork right, plus the first submitted invoice carried an incorrect amount resulting in further payment delay, which antagonised Brown resulting in the derogatory letter. The committee members and the Director General were extremely annoyed, which they made both the agent Thaitek and myself aware of.

Brown would never learn. I telephoned him and explained the volatile situation he had created and advised that it would be wise to withdraw his letter and to my surprise, he agreed.

After the letter was withdrawn, both committee vice chairman Piboon and Capt. Chitepong asked me if I would come and discuss with them any future nasty shitty letters from Brown before official submittal.

The construction of the three Dredgers in the New Orleans shipyard was not progressing as expected, falling way behind schedule due to Brown's lack of progress payments. No money, no work, was the motto of the shipyard. At one point, the shipyard had not worked on the Dredgers for a month due to lack of payment, and to re-mobilise it cost Brown an extra half million dollars. Rivers told me Brown would be wiser to pay them off and bring the project back to Sasco's yard in Thailand, however he never mentioned that to Brown.

Rivers suggested that Brown and Dr Pryor were not on good terms, as Brown figured Pryor was not representing Eastern as per the terms of their contract and the monthly agreement. He also told me Brown was worried about an audit by the Trade and Development Agency representatives in Washington DC, as the $100,000 under the table commission was in fact misappropriation of United States government training funds for developing countries.

Finally, after the controversy faded and Thaitek's promise to pay under the table commissions to the Director General and committee members, and the passing of two months from the original invoice submittal date, the $7.5 million keel lay payment was received by Eastern. I also received three months unpaid expenses plus Rivers had transferred to me $5,000 from his secret 'slush fund'. When it rains, it pours!

Slowly, as the months rolled by, the thirty-inch Dredger hulls being constructed in the New Orleans shipyard began to take shape. Each Dredger was fitted with two power drive units. One unit was a single Caterpillar engine to drive the generator and produce all electrical power requirements. The second power unit was two Caterpillar engines, connected in tandem. These engines drive through a gearbox, which is connected to the thirty-inch diameter Dredger pump that sucks all material that is dredged up by the forward rotary cutter.

The material is sucked through a thirty-inch diameter pipe into the center opening of the pump by the spinning pump internal impeller. It is then jettisoned through a discharge outlet into the Floating Pipeline system ending up as landfill or dumped in the ocean where it does not interfere with shipping lanes.

Eastern had placed an order with the Caterpillar representatives in Baltimore for all engines. As ordered, the first engines arrived on schedule. These were the engines that would drive the generator for electrical power.

As far as Eastern was concerned, these engines were classified as the Dredger's 'main engines'. That related to the milestone payment 'shipment of main engines', worth $7.5 million. Eastern submitted the invoice for payment. Several weeks later, it was rejected with the explanation that the inspection committee considered the tandem engines that powered the Dredger pumps as the 'main engines'.

This put Eastern in a bind as the tandem engines were a minimum of six months away from delivery and Eastern was once again in a monetary debacle—they had no friggen cash.

Facsimiles, letters and meetings between the committee, Eastern and their agent Thaitek were happening in an attempt to resolve the problem. The internal politics of the Ports and Rivers Authority kicked in and the Inspection Committee requested and received documentation to support Eastern's interpretation of 'main engines', including a letter from the Classification Society, the American Bureau of Shipping. Finally, Thaitek's Dr Pryor informed Brown that the Inspection Committee requested $300,000 as under the table commission for approval. Pryor explained the payments had been scheduled for $150,000 after Eastern had received the milestone payment 'shipment of main engines' and the remaining $150,000 after the milestone payment 'shipment of Dredge pump and gearbox'. Brown agreed and Pryor waited for another wire transfer of cash to his Singapore account.

I received a telephone call from the Sasco shipyard, requesting I visit their facilities regarding a kick-off meeting for construction of the Tender Boats. During the meeting, I was informed that the contract for design of the boats was given to Vice Chairman Piboon of the Inspection Committee. Piboon was a partner in a small naval architecture consulting company.

Of course, this situation could be construed as a conflict of interest, as he would be inspecting and approving his own work as a member of the committee and an employee of the Ports and Rivers Authority. However, that is locally known as 'Thai Style' or 'Mai Mee Phan Ha' (No problem!).

Rivers sent me an email explaining that Eastern had sub-contracted a foundry in South Korea for the Dredger hull pumps and impellers. There were a total of eighteen castings, one pump, one impeller, plus two spares of each item per Dredger. The email stated, owing to the South Korean economic crash, that they were doing the work at cost price, no profit. This was a saving of three million dollars for Eastern over US foundries. Rivers advised me that the first three sets of castings would be ready for inspection within four to six weeks and he would require me to visit the Korean facilities for the purpose of approval and acceptance before shipment.

The contract between Eastern and the Ports and Rivers Authority had several clauses regarding manufacturers and origin of goods, which read,

"The seller (Eastern Dredging Co.) shall provide the buyer (Ports and Rivers Authority) with a manufacturer's certificate of origin for all goods, stating the country where the goods were manufactured, and the manufacturer's name and address. Also, all major items of equipment are to be from suppliers acceptable to the buyer."

Eastern never informed the Ports and Rivers Authority of any manufacturers they were utilising for equipment, meaning the Ports and Rivers Authority never had the opportunity to approve or disapprove.

During a previous meeting with the inspection committee, Brown informed them that a foundry in the US—that Eastern was utilising—was having labor union problems, and the workers had gone on strike, which would cause a delay with some Dredger items.

The Chairman of the Inspection Committee asked, 'Is this the foundry where the Dredger pumps and impellers were being cast?'

Both Brown and Rivers responded, 'Yes, indeed.'

Later that day, Rivers and myself met in the Committee Chairman's office along with Vice Chairman Piboon and Captain Chitepong. During the course of conversation regarding the thirty-inch Dredger project, Rivers told the gathering, 'I never lie to the client, never have, never will.' I thought to myself, what a fucking hypocrite!

A month rolled by and it was time to depart Thailand and go on a foundry inspection trip to Inchon, South Korea. Several weeks before leaving, Rivers had told me to make sure no one at Eastern's agent Thaitek or the inspection committee had any idea where I was going. I told everyone I would be in Singapore for a couple of days R and R. All foundry items, after acceptance, would be shipped to Los Angeles, California. There they would be uncrated and any and all Korean markings would be removed. They would then be re-crated for shipment to Thailand and one set of each sent to the New Orleans shipyard for installation into the Dredgers.

Eastern's reasoning for not shipping directly to Thailand from South Korea was, of course, avoidance of contractual infringement.

They would have to produce fraudulent documentation stating all manufacture was in the US. Eastern did this for a specific reason, contractually; all cost savings were to be passed back to the Ports and Rivers Authority. There was no way Brown was going to share his profits.

CHAPTER 12

ANOTHER KEEL LAY CEREMONY at Sasco, this time for the Tender Boats. In attendance were the Director General and an entourage of approximately thirty personnel, including the Inspection Committee. Thaitek's Dr Pryor had assured me the previous day he would also be in attendance, however no Thaitek personnel showed. Some of the committee asked me where they were and said as Eastern's Thai agent, they should be in attendance.

I agreed with the committee members, suggesting that maybe they were hung-up in the heavily congested Bangkok traffic, but I was beginning to think that Thaitek weren't as honest and truthful as I first thought. During the ceremony the owner of Sasco, Khun Mechi approached me and we had a short discussion about Eastern and the thirty-inch Dredger project with him, saying that if Brown had left the project with Sasco, the Dredgers would be nearing completion instead of heading into what may be heavy duty penalties. He then said to me, 'Brown is too young for his position, he must be taught a lesson.' Brown was forty–three years old.

After leaving the keel lay ceremony at Sasco and driving several blocks in the Isuzu pick-up, it started to chug-a-lug like an old coal-burning train, this wasn't the first time I'd had this problem and knew exactly what to do. Almost on a monthly basis, I had to drain the diesel fuel system because of water contamination. Adulteration of motor fuels was a constant problem in Thailand as was fuel oil smuggling, according to a report by the Royal Thai Police Office at least two billion litres are smuggled into the country each year. Unscrupulous gasoline and diesel fuel dealers were blending their products with solvents as well as water. The Excise Department, because of consumer complaints, claimed to have cracked down on the dealers, but the Isuzu 'monthlies' were still occurring.

I reported to Rivers on the successful progress of the twenty-inch Dredger project. The twenty-inch Inspection Committee had visited the Prakarn Joint Venture Shipyard for a milestone inspection of the hull completion, and was impressed with the quality and quantity of work. It was becoming obvious to me after analysing both projects, that the process of doing business in Thailand produced a lot less heartache and headaches when the involvement was through a joint venture.

Every problem that I had encountered with the twenty-inch project had been dealt with on a basis of a Thai negotiating with a Thai, and was solved with a lot of talking but a minimum of fuss and expense.

Things were not going well with the thirty-inch project. Letters officially submitted by Eastern to the inspection committee requesting acceptance of several changed technical items were returned, asking for more details and manufacturer's catalogues. The committee was playing hardball but at the same time, they were covering their asses.

Brown was having problems of his own. I received an 11.30 am telephone call from him, which meant it was 11.30 pm his time. He told me he had been having a telephone conversation with his agent Dr Pryor of Thaitek, and Pryor had hung up on him.

The Thaitek agency was not living up to its end of the bargain, he continued he would not pay them any more money until the completion of the project. He had wire transferred $400,000 that day to their Singapore account and now they had told him they required another $800,000. Also Thaitek had, in Brown's mind, done nothing to obtain an extension of time for the Dredgers to be completed.

All they wanted was money. He told me to go and speak with Capt. Chitepong and Vice Chairman Piboon and try to find out if Thaitek had paid the large under the table commissions as claimed.

Contractually, Eastern had a total of 540 days from date of execution of the contract to deliver the Dredgers to Thailand, there were approximately 150 days left until the official delivery date. The Dredgers would require at least another six months for completion after the cut-off date. This was the time extension Brown believed Thaitek would secure, but hadn't.

Every day past the final delivery date, Eastern would be liable for penalty charges of $50,000 per day. The penalty costs could not exceed ten percent of the contract price. The next step would be contract termination by the buyer.

Several minutes after my telephone conversation with Brown ended, I received another call, this time it was Terdsak telling me Dr Pryor had a problem with Brown; we arranged a meeting that afternoon at Thaitek's office for further discussion.

I met with Pryor and two of his loyal employees; they were

pissed off big time, telling me about how much of their own hard-earned cash they had spent on Brown's behalf, paying under the table commissions to government and the inspection people. All Brown did was upset the Thai officials with nasty letters, plus he had utilised the US Embassy's Commercial Section for his support, but Dr Pryor's biggest concern was Brown not transferring reimbursement money.

I told them Brown had informed me that he had just wire transferred $400,000. They agreed he had, but told me they had paid out a further $800,000 and if that amount was not in their Singapore account within twenty–four hours, then the party was over.

Dr Pryor told me he would inform all Ports and Rivers Authority personnel and government ministers that his company, Thaitek, no longer represented Eastern, and the reason for terminating the relationship was the lack of receiving promised funds.

My experience with Eastern's late salary and expense payments had me believing what the Thaitek people were telling me. I had, at that time, no cause to doubt them, and asked Dr Pryor if he could delay speaking to anyone about the current problem until I spoke with Brown that night to see if I could convince him to pay up. Pryor readily agreed, as the cash register rang in his head.

My telephone call with Brown lasted twenty minutes. I impressed upon him how important it was to keep Thaitek on our side, that without them, Eastern would be in a world of shit. Finally, he stated he would wire transfer no less than $200,000 but it would not be anywhere near $800,000. The following day at Thaitek's office, I learned the actual amount of the transfer into Dr Pryor's Singapore account was $480,000.00. Pryor advised he would remain as Eastern's representative and as he had only received fifty percent of what he required, he would inform all recipients of future under the table commissions that they would only receive fifty percent. The reason was Eastern's failure to forward sufficient funds. I was thinking, you cheap motherfucker, because of my efforts you received almost half a million dollars and you didn't even bother to buy me a cup of coffee, let alone lunch.

Pryor was also complaining about the Inspection Committee Vice Chairman Piboon and Capt. Chitepong. 'Money is all they are interested in,' he said, 'every time I see them they are asking for money; they want to know when they will get their $300,000 for the Eastern milestone payments.' Pryor also stated how he was lobbying Director General Allrot to have Piboon removed from the committee and also Chitepong if possible; he figured that would solve all problems.

Well I'd heard it all before, months earlier, but both Piboon and Chitepong were still in their original positions. Later that day I had a telephone conversation with Brown and explained the Dr Pryor rhetoric, Brown became agitated and told me he would facsimile me copies of the wire transfers he had made to Pryor's Singapore account. He then told me to show them to either Vice Chairman Piboon or Capt. Chitepong, whomever I felt more comfortable with, or show both of them if I wished. This would prove that monies had been transferred for under the table commissions.

During my travels around the streets of Bangkok from shipyard to shipyard, from Thaitek's office to the Royal Orchard hotel, the sight of elephants waddling in and out of traffic never ceased to amaze me. As the Thai agriculture and lumber industries became mechanised, the elephant, which had been utilised as the prime mover or power source, had become redundant. The Mahouts, who were the driver or keeper of the elephants, were bringing their massive animals to town, hoping for government assistance and to eke out a living from the locals and tourists. In Thailand, the elephant is a sacred beast in a very special way—it figures in the religious culture and in Buddha's birth story. It is central to Thai Royal history as military equipment, parade transportation and as a magical protector of the realm represented by the 'White Elephant'. The elephant is much more than a religious and royal icon; they are loved and revered by all Thai people for their unique combination of power and vulnerability.

Just how vulnerable they are was exposed when thirty veterinarians spent more than three hours operating on a twenty-year-old cow elephant whose left foreleg was severely damaged after she stepped on a landmine while foraging for food in the forests along the Thai-Burma border. A crane was needed to hoist the 2,700 kilogram elephant onto a specially-constructed operating table and enough anaesthetic to floor seventy humans had to be administered before the operation could begin. Medical experts including surgeons, anaesthesiologists and orthopaedists fitted an artificial leg, which today is allowing the elephant to live an almost normal life.

CHAPTER 13

THE TWENTY-INCH COMMITTEE, HEADED by Capt. Chitepong visited the Prakarn Joint Venture Shipyard for a further progress inspection visit. They were very happy with what they inspected. Capt. Chitepong was not happy with Eastern's performance regarding the thirty-inch project and told me, 'This is the first and last Ports and Rivers Authority contract for Eastern.' I didn't find it hard to understand why he made such a comment but there was fuck all I could do to change things.

During the inspection visit, I received a telephone call from Thaitek's Dr Pryor. He told me not to worry about the thirty-inch project. He stated that he and his assistant Terdsak had met with Director General Allrot. As a result of the meeting, the Director General had told him that Vice Chairman Piboon and Capt. Chitepong, who Pryor had been saying for a long time were the reason for all the problems, would have their power curtailed, and only he and the Committee Chairman would be the decision-makers. Dr Pryor continued that he had informed the Director General that both Piboon and Chitepong had been collecting $100 per day from each of the Ports and Rivers Authority inspectors stationed in the United States, which infuriated Director General Allrot. Pryor then told me his agency had paid under the table commissions of 16 million Baht to two government ministers and 32 million Baht to one other minister. Also, the Director General had received 4 million Baht and both Piboon and Chitepong, 1 million Baht each.

As Chairman of the Training Committee, Chitepong had also received $20,000 of his requested $100,000 under the table commission from the Trade and Development Agency Grant. I figured with all that money being handed out, just maybe Pryor had solved the problems. But that's the thing about life; most of it is based on deception.

A couple of weeks later, the inspection Committee along with several of Thaitek's employees were arranging to visit the New Orleans shipyard to view the progress of the thirty-inch Dredgers. US entrance visas were required before departure; I supplied, on Eastern letterhead, 'Letters of Visa Request' for each individual, which had to be presented at the visa section of the US embassy on Wireless Road in Bangkok. I was at the Royal Orchid at seven am to meet Thaitek's Khun Preecha and travel with him and several Ports and Rivers Authority personnel to the Embassy when I received a telephone call from Capt. Chitepong asking if I could visit him in his office.

A short ten-minute walk and I was in his office. He seemed despondent, telling me he had been given some information regarding Eastern that disturbed him but wanted to investigate further and asked me to join him for lunch to discuss it in more detail. I agreed to meet with him later and left to visit the US embassy.

During the visa application process, I told Thaitek's

Preecha I would be having lunch with Chitepong, he immediately made a telephone call which was obviously to his controller, then he asked me if he could join the luncheon engagement, I told him, 'Up to you.'

After lunch in a quaint Chinese restaurant located in a small Soi near the Ports and Rivers Authority building, I began walking towards the Royal Orchid Hotel where I had parked the Isuzu. As only general conversation regarding the upcoming US trip was discussed during lunch, Preecha left for his office believing it had been only a social event. However, Capt. Chitepong joined me saying he had business in the general direction of the Royal Orchid.

As we neared the Hotel, Chitepong asked if I'd join him for coffee, he said he had something to discuss, but didn't want to discuss it at lunch in front of Thaitek personnel. After the coffee was served, Chitepong stated that the two inspectors in New Orleans had telephoned both he and committee Vice Chairman Piboon telling them that Rivers had been making statements that Eastern was paying hundreds of thousands of dollars to the committee members.

I responded by saying, 'It is my understanding, according to Thaitek's Dr Pryor, that you guys on the committee have received a bunch of cash and are expecting more. To be precise, you requested and received $150,000 for the milestone acceptance for 'shipment of main engines' and you are expecting another $150,000 on your acceptance of the milestone 'shipment of Dredge pump and gear box'.' Chitepong seemed flabbergasted at this statement.

He told me he didn't know if Director General Allrot had received any money but no member of the committee had received any payment. In fact Thaitek's Terdsak had approached both himself and Piboon and offered $40,000 for the acceptance for 'shipment of main engines' but there

101

had never been any discussion regarding the milestone 'shipment of Dredge pump and gear box'. I asked him if Thaitek had paid him the $20,000 from the requested $100,000 of the Trade and Development Agency grant, he admitted they had and he volunteered that Khun Savit, owner of the Joint Venture Shipyard - Prakarn, had paid him a commission of half million Baht, as he was the chairman of the Inspection Committee for the twenty-inch project.

We had been in conversation about an hour when my mobile rang and it was Thaitek's Preecha asking me what Chitepong wanted. I acted dumb and told him that he had been at lunch and had heard the conversation, he said no, not lunch, as he had seen Chitepong join me on my way back to the Royal Orchid Hotel. I told him when we neared the Hotel, I went my way and Chitepong his, end of story, which he accepted and hung up.

I told Chitepong that people at Thaitek must be worried; they were just checking on whether he and I were together. Preecha's telephone call encouraged Chitepong to lay it all on the table.

He explained that Dr Pryor had visited with the Director General many times and stated that Brown was a bad guy, he would promise money transfers for under the table commissions but never delivered. Chitepong added that the Director General sympathised with Pryor and agreed that Brown was no good.

I decided it was time to show Chitepong evidence that Brown had in fact sent commission monies to Pryor and handed him the three facsimiles of the wire transfers, which showed amounts of $150,000, $243,000 and $480,000.

Chitepong asked for copies so he could show the committee members and the Director General, figuring this evidence would prove that Dr Pryor and his people were liars and it should produce an attitude change and a better working relationship could develop between Eastern and themselves.

Chitepong continued that the original bid committee and the previous Director General who had assisted, evaluated and approved the project being awarded to Eastern, had been promised under the table commissions by Thaitek people but had never received any payment. He said he knew that Eastern had assisted the Thaitek agency in becoming the Thailand representative of an American buoy manufacturer and that Thaitek had learned of the Ports and Rivers Authority's requirement for several thousand marker-buoys to be utilised in the local shipping lanes. This led to Dr Pryor inviting the committee, which had been set up within the Ports and Rivers Authority to investigate the purchase of the buoys, to an evening dinner.

Several members of this newly-organised buoy purchasing committee had been on the old Dredger bid committee.

Halfway through the dinner, Dr Pryor and his people raised the issue of supplying the buoys with promises of under the table commission. Hearing these similar money promises and remembering the past, the invited personnel stood up, excused themselves and left the dinner.

Chitepong also told me that both he and Piboon had been questioned by Director General Allrot regarding the $100 per day they had been receiving from the Inspectors in the United States. The Director General told them that Thaitek had given him the information; he then ordered them to pay the money back, which was now up to US $20,000 each, and in future treat their subordinates with the respect they deserve. A huge 'loss of face' for both individuals, he added that he and Piboon wanted revenge regarding Thaitek, but were not sure how to go about it without hurting Eastern. At the conclusion of our conversation, Chitepong made the statement, 'To prove that Thaitek was being factious and to clear the air, the best thing to do was to have Rivers and or Brown, myself, Thaitek's Dr Pryor and members of the inspection committee sit down and lay all cards on the table regarding commission payments.'

We went to the hotel's business center and took photocopies of the wire transfers Chitepong had requested and then parted. I advised Rivers by telephone and email, the only response was, he wasn't surprised and that he would discuss it further with Brown.

Several days later, I was at Thaitek's office and decided to speak with Dr Pryor. I asked him if he had the committee members sign anything stating they had received commission payments. He said, 'No! They could go to jail for that.'

So I responded, 'Then it's your word against theirs.'

His brown face flushed pink and his voice rose several octaves as he told me, 'You can check with the government ministers, I pay them, I don't care what those low life committee scumbags say, I pay them all!'

I stood up to leave his office and told him, 'It's no good getting angry with me; I am only trying to look after Eastern's interest.' Although I didn't know it then, that was to be my last visit to Thaitek's office.

Several hours later, Capt. Chitepong telephoned me and said that he and the other committee members had just left the office of Director General Allrot who had informed them that Thaitek's Dr Pryor had just given him $50,000 to be spread among the committee members.

That evening Rivers telephoned and told me Dr Pryor had called him and advised him to tell me not to listen to gossip, and with regard to the $150,000 payments—well $40,000 of each of the two payments was for the committee members and the two payments of $110,000 was for the Director General. Pryor's story was changing to suit the circumstances.

Rivers also asked for an update regarding the thirteen blueprint drawings I had submitted several months earlier in June for the thirty-inch Dredgers. As it was now November, the month of Loy Kratong in Thailand, he figured sufficient time had passed for approval. These were the drawings I had mistakenly submitted under the twenty-inch project.

I visited Piboon and asked about the status of the drawings. He searched his office but couldn't find them, he telephoned several other internal departments but 'they could not be found nowhere'. In addition, the Ports and Rivers Authority submittal log showed no record of their submittal. Piboon advised me to re-submit a set of drawings and that he would personally hurry their approval. I contacted Rivers, told him the saga and requested he courier a new set, which he agreed to do. The following week I received them but there was a difference—in the original set there were thirteen, the new set contained fourteen.

Contractually all technical changes, such as substituting electrical motors, pumps, cable sizes or other items from the original specifications had to be submitted to the Inspection Committee to obtain approval. Support documentation relating to manufacturer's catalogues proving the item was equivalent or superior to the original specified item in the contract bid documents, had to be submitted. Any cost savings were to be passed back to the Ports and Rivers Authority. I checked the new set of fourteen blueprint drawings and realised Eastern had changed many technical items without the inspection committee approval. These changes created the extra drawing. The following day I submitted them but I did not inform Piboon of the technical changes.

Possibly the most romantic festival of the Thai calendar

occurs with the full moon in November. The 'Loy Krathong' festival dates back around seven hundred years, it is based on a Hindu tradition of thanking the water Goddess and it marks the end of the rainy season and the main rice harvest. 'Loy' means to float, while 'Krathong' means a Lotus-shaped vessel usually made of banana tree leaves. The Krathong vessel usually contains a candle, three incense sticks, flowers and a few coins. The candle and incense are lit, a wish is made and the Krathong is launched. It is believed the Krathong can carry away sins and bad luck, if the candle remains burning until the Krathong is out of sight the wish will come true, however this is not always possible as Krathongs are launched on canals, rivers, small ponds and even swimming pools. It is a special evening to see the hundreds of lit-up Krathongs floating on the waters, supplemented by fireworks and the Thai females, who all dress in their finest woven native silk.

CHAPTER 14

WHEN THE THIRTY-INCH DREDGERS were completed in New Orleans, they would have to be transported to Thailand. The mode of transportation would be as either self-propelled heavy lift vessel or several large barges, which would be towed by an ocean-going tugboat. The fifty-meter long by fourteen-meter wide Dredges would be loaded on the deck of the transport vessel and several months after leaving New Orleans, they would arrive in Bangkok.

The cost of carrying the Dredges from the United States to Thailand ranged from $1.5 up to $2.5 million dollars. Rivers asked me to check around and find out what vessels would be available. On one of my regular Saturday visits to the Prakarn Joint Venture Shipyard, I enlisted the assistance of the now Admiral Somboon who had recently been promoted from Captain. Admiral Somboon had contacts in Singapore and asked me how much Rivers and I would require as an under the table commission payment.

Once again I was surprised by the request, but I told the good Admiral I would discuss it with Rivers, which I did and the following Saturday advised him that Rivers had authorised a dollar loading, $150,000—$100,000 for me and $50,000 for himself. The Singapore price with our graft plus Admiral Somboon's was $2.75 million. Rivers thought this amount was too high and told me to advise Admiral Somboon that during his next visit to Bangkok in December, we would all visit Singapore to negotiate the price down. He also advised me that draftsman Ted would be in Bangkok after an inspection visit to the foundry at Inchon, South Korea. Rivers asked me if I had arranged to have Ted photographed in a sexual situation, I told him, 'Maybe, I am still working on it.' In fact, I had done nothing. Rivers also told me he wanted me to be at the shipyard in New Orleans in a couple of months. He had the Vice President of Eastern's Human Resources Department fax me a letter to obtain a business visa.

I received a telephone call from Thaitek's Dr Pryor, advising me that he had been having meetings with Director General Allrot and the news was that due to his lobbying, both Vice Chairman Piboon and Capt. Chitepong would be removed from the thirty-inch project Inspection Committee before the end of December. Sarcastically I asked him, 'Which year?' I mean this guy was forever shovelling the same shit.

I called Chitepong and told him of my conversation with Pryor. His response was, 'If that's what the Director General wants then that's the way it will be, mi mee phan ha.' adding it was now time for the 'Empire to Strike Back'. He, Piboon and several other committee members were going to have payback. I told him, if there was anyway I could help, let me know.

Several weeks later Ted arrived in Bangkok. This guy always had an attitude of self-importance. When he questioned me about certain aspects of the two Dredger projects regarding circumstances that I felt were of no concern to him,

I would stall him by advising that it was best he discuss it with Rivers. His second day in Bangkok I was driving him to the Sasco shipyard for a progress inspection of the Tender Boats, when I asked him if that evening he would like to visit 'Ground Zero' of the sex industry in Bangkok, to which he readily agreed.

Seven o'clock that evening I hailed a taxi out front of the Royal Orchid Hotel and told the driver to take us to the 'Nana Plaza', Soi 4 Nana Tai, Sukhumvit Road. The Plaza was directly across the street from the old 'Nana Hotel' which legend has it, was the unofficial headquarters of the American CIA during the Vietnam War. Bangkok inner city traffic that time of the evening is unbelievable. We were stuck in a jam and going nowhere, Ted asked how much farther, I told him if he wished we could walk, it wouldn't be more than twenty minutes, so I paid the eighty Baht cab fare.

When we reached the 'Nana Plaza', Ted asked why it was called 'Ground Zero' I replied, 'Cause this is where it all happens man, just follow me and you will understand.'

The 'Nana Plaza' consists of three floors built in a 'U' shape, the ground in the center of the building used to be a parking lot, but now, like every floor it is occupied with beer bars, A-Go-Go bars, rooms for rent by the hour and male and female sex industry workers. I walked up the stairs with Ted close on my heels, turned a couple of corners, passed by the ever popular expatriate bar, 'The Hog's Breath', and found the bar I was looking for on the second floor, called 'Naughty Boys'.

Thailand has some of the world's most beautiful transvestites or Katoeys, (lady boys) as they are called in Thai, many having had complete sex change operations and due to hormonal and other treatments, they all have enlarged breasts. In a recent 'Miss Queen of the Universe' contest that was held at the Wiltshire Grand Hotel in Los Angeles, competitors from over forty countries competed for the most beautiful 'Woman of the Second Category' to be crowned Miss Queen of the Universe. Thailand's own, Ms Phatriya from Pattaya City won the crown.

A beer bar ran along the wall to the left as you entered 'Naughty Boys', low couches and tables to the right. We sat on a couch and immediately several of the scantily clad bar workers joined us. I arranged the seating so as to have one on Ted's left and one on his right, another squatted in front of the low table and I ordered drinks all around. Ted immediately put his arm around the shoulders of the individual to his left and began exploring the exposed midriff flesh with his free hand. I gave a hundred Baht to each of the other two Katoeys, and told them to kiss Ted full on the lips, which they did. Ted was enjoying himself, and asked what I was doing to him, I responded, 'Showing you a good time man.'

I whispered to the Katoey on Ted's right, 'Grab his dick.'

The Katoey asked, 'Does he know what we are?'

'Don't worry, it's okay, he won't hurt you.' Inside the dimly lit bar it was almost impossible to define true images and Ted had no idea, his hands and mouth were working overtime and he was exploring the breasts of his companion.

I watched, trying hard not to laugh as his hand moved slowly back and forth across his newfound friend's bare midriff. With each movement, it inched lower towards the groin area and eventually his fingers slipped under the top of the bikini briefs, his companion immediately kissed Ted full on the lips. During the lip lock, Ted's hand made it all the way to his kissing friend's dick. In one swift movement, Ted tore his lips from his companion and withdrew his hand with such force that his right leg flew into the air, connecting with the low table sending it and the glasses of beer flying and the Katoey's screaming. Ted jumped to his feet, I was almost hysterical, from somewhere in the darkened bar, two huge Thai men had Ted by each arm. He hollered, 'Help me out here man!' In my broken Thai I explained to the two bouncers it was okay and Ted would pay everyone money. I then told Ted he would have to pay each person one thousand Baht and, 'Mi me phan ha' (no problem). Rivers had told me Ted didn't like to part with his money but he paid up and we left the 'Naughty Boys' bar.

Ted wanted no more Bangkok nightlife, so we caught a taxi back to the Royal Orchid Hotel. During the journey, he said to me, 'Do me a favour man, don't tell no one about tonight.'

I responded by telling him, 'Ted, there's something you have to learn, and that is, love and war do not follow the ordinary rules of life.'

The following day I sent Rivers an email describing draftsman Ted's adventure, hoping that would be satisfactory, even though I had no photographs for support.

CHAPTER 15

THE CONTRACT BETWEEN EASTERN and Sasco stated that all payments were due within ten days of satisfactory completion of milestones and associated documentation. If the payments were late, interest would be charged at the rate of eight percent per annum—compounded daily. Brown was two months late paying Sasco for the Tender Boat keel lay payment of $1.4 million. He sent me an email telling me he had sent a cheque by an international courier service and when I received it, I was to deliver it to Sasco. That same day I visited Sasco and took several photographs of the progress of the Tender Boats and then joined Sasco's Boat Construction Manager, Bluey, an Australian, in his field-site office.

We were discussing his progress and that of the thirty-inch Dredgers; he told me Sasco were concerned about the keel lay payment. I told him of the email I had received that morning and if Brown was telling the truth (which you never knew when it came to him paying his bills); I should have the cheque in three days. I had no sooner finished speaking of the payment when the office door opened and Sasco's MD

Chang and his assistant Suwat, entered. Before I could speak, MD Chang, with a flushed face and a raised voice hollered, 'Where's my money? Brown's lawyer said I would have it one week ago, where's my money?' Before I could answer, Chang asked Bluey if I had been given any documents, he was told 'no.' Chang then ordered me off his property, saying I was not an authorised representative of Eastern and to get off his property immediately. This was extremely unusual conduct for a Thai to raise his voice in anger, especially at a foreigner; it represented in the Thai culture a huge 'loss of face'.

Listed in the Eastern/Sasco contract were two people as Eastern representatives—Rivers and Brown. Several months earlier, Sasco had sent a fax to Baltimore requesting my name be included as the local Eastern representative, but the folk in Baltimore had let it slip. Consequently, I had no contractual right, so I told Chang I would inform Eastern that I had been ordered out of his shipyard, Chang's response was he didn't give a fiddler's fuck what I told Eastern, all he wanted was his money. As I was picking up my camera, I told Chang that I had only that morning received an email explaining about the cheque coming by courier.

I headed towards the office door and Chang made a move towards me as though he was going to interfere with my movement and asked, 'Did you take any photographs?'

I immediately went on the defensive, 'If you think you are going to touch this camera, you had better think again.'

He stopped, but I could see he was furious. As I walked the hundred yards to my vehicle, I asked assistant Suwat, who up to now had not said a word, what he wanted me to do with the cheque when it arrived, as I was now barred from entering the shipyard. There was no response. I left the shipyard, parked out on the street and telephoned Rivers, getting him out of bed. He apologised and promised to correct the matter, saying he would send a fax to Sasco naming me as an Eastern representative.

Two days later the cheque arrived, I telephoned the owner of Sasco, Khun Mechi and advised him I had received the keel lay payment by courier, and what did he want me to do with it as his nephew, MD Chang had ordered me out of the shipyard. Khun Mechi said he was sorry about the actions of Chang, but he was under a lot of pressure, he then asked me why I worked for a crook like Brown.

I told him I had been looking for a new employer for several months but so far no luck and, I added, every month I had to badger Eastern for my salary and expenses. He seemed surprised at this statement and arranged to meet in a couple of hours for lunch to receive the cheque, then hung up. Fifteen minutes later, he called me back and asked how much the cheque was. When I told him he said it was the wrong amount, that Brown had not included the eight percent interest therefore he could not accept the cheque, also the lunch date was cancelled, asking me to advise Brown to wire transfer the correct amount, and not mess around with couriered cheques. I told him I would, what else could I say, it wasn't worth worrying about things I had no control over.

Early in the New Year both Brown and Rivers arrived in Bangkok. This time they stayed at the 'Rama Garden Hotel' in the Bangkok suburb of Don Muang about ten kilometres from the International Airport and a five-minute drive from the agent Thaitek's office.

Prior to his arrival Brown had submitted the invoice for milestone payment, shipment of Dredge pump and gearbox. In his estimation the inspection committee, whose duty it was to authorise payment, were late. With the assistance of Thaitek, he had again submitted a nasty shitty letter, upsetting the complete Ports and Rivers Authority contingent connected to the thirty-inch project. Prior to their arrival, I had received, by International courier, a package of letters and affidavits and submitted them to the inspection committee. The subject—'Force Majeure'. Eastern was trying to make up lost time; they were using inclement winter weather and industrial strike action, which had occurred at one of the US foundries utilised for manufacturing of Dredger parts.

They were requesting fifty–eight days contract extension due to 'Force Majeure' delays. In fact, the strike and the weather combined had caused no more than a fourteen-day delay.

The Chief Notary and Authentication Section of the District of Columbia (Washington DC) had signed one affidavit. One of the letters supporting the affidavit bore the title: United States of America, Department of State. It carried the paragraph,

"I, Madeleine K. Albright, Secretary of State, have hereunto caused the seal of the Department of State to be affixed and my name subscribed by the Authentication Officer of the said department, at the city of Washington, in the District of Columbia."

It was dated and bore two signatures, that of Madeleine K. Albright and the Assistant Authentication Officer, Department of State.

Brown was trying to impress or frighten the Thais with his political connections. After submittal and discussions I had with the committee members, he had only impressed himself, the Thais certainly were not. Brown had learned nothing regarding the Thai psyche.

Brown, through the commercial section of the US embassy had arranged a meeting with Deputy Minister Sanit of the

Shipping and Commerce Government Ministry. He, Rivers and Dr Pryor were trying to obtain a construction extension of eight months to allow completion of the thirty-inch Dredgers, and to not be liable for the $5 million penalties. According to Rivers, the Deputy Minister listened to Brown explain his problems but did not seem too concerned, he then canvassed Brown regarding certain aspects of the US government system including President Clinton's impeachment problems. Rivers said that Brown became hostile and sarcastic and finished up insulting Deputy Minister Sanit, seemed Brown was in character.

A luncheon invitation was extended by Brown and Pryor to Sanit, however as they were about to depart his office, Sasco's owner Khun Mechi arrived for what was apparently a weekly luncheon engagement with the Deputy Minister, who excused himself from the Brown/Pryor offer and left with Khun Mechi. Rivers told me when Brown sighted Khun Mechi he was rude and brushed off Khun Mechi's handshake—another mistake.

That evening, a dinner was arranged with Director General Allrot, the Inspection Committee and four Thaitek agency people. During the dinner, Director General Allrot received a telephone call from Minister Annop, who was Deputy Minister Sanit's boss. I learned later that Minister Annop was pissed off big time. As his office had received a request from the Commercial Attaché at the US embassy asking for a meeting, Annop asked, 'Who is this guy Brown?'

After all the shit Brown was pulling and his contempt for the Thais as a client, the inspection Committee members, in their congenial Thai nature, invited Brown, Rivers and myself to join them on a boat trip the following day along the Chao Phraya River. Halfway through the trip we tied up to a jetty connected to a huge boathouse where the Royal Barges were housed.

As far back as the Fourteenth century, during the eleventh lunar month, the Thais have held a race called the 'Asayucha Ceremony'; a predicative race between the King and Queen's barges. According to custom, if the Queen's barge won, the country would enjoy prosperity, however if the King's barge won, disaster would ensue. In the mid seventeen hundreds when the then Thai capital city of Ayutthaya fell to Burma, hundreds of elegant Royal barges were burnt to the waterline by invading Burmese soldiers, which historically, is one of Thailand's greatest national tragedies. The barges sat idle for many years. In 1951, after returning to Thailand from his overseas studies, His Majesty, King Bhumibol Adulyadej (Rama IX), inspected the Royal barges at their dry dock in Bangkok Noi canal, requesting the barges be restored and their ceremonies revived as both were an integral part of Thai heritage. A recent Royal Barge procession along the Chao Phraya, River of Kings, occurred in a spectacular tribute to mark His Majesty, The King's sixth cycle or seventy–second birthday. Fifty–three exquisitely carved and elaborately decorated barges were on display, each manned by fifty oarsmen, two helmsmen, two officers, one flagman and a timekeeper, the rowers raising their silver and gold paddles together at the end of each stroke in rhythm with the timekeeper, who tapped the butt of a silver spear on the deck. More than two thousand Royal Thai Navy sailors manned the barges.

Our tour of the Chao Phraya river ended at noon and we had lunch at a Thai restaurant called 'Yokyor' which is situated on the opposite river bank to the Ports and Rivers Authority headquarters and the Royal Orchid Hotel. Considering the annoyance in the hearts of the Thai committee members regarding Brown's nasty shitty letter implying payment improprieties and his caustic attitude, they were perfect hosts. At the completion of lunch, we crossed the river by local ferry and Brown, Rivers and myself were escorted by Capt. Chitepong to his office, where for the next forty–five minutes, Chitepong discussed the two Dredger projects and described the lies and innuendoes of Eastern's agent Thaitek. Brown wasn't listening, instead he stupidly raised the issue of the committee members walking out on the dinner engagement in New Orleans, which happened months earlier and was now history.

I strongly believed by now that Brown was a complete self-centred fuckwit, he did not even have the courtesy to accept that the Ports and Rivers Authority personnel were in fact the client, the owner of the end product—the Dredgers his company was constructing. They were paying him for a service and instead of trying to understand their problems; all he wanted to do was argue and in his sarcastic manner only succeeded in vilifying himself. During the whole forty–five minutes Rivers sat and never uttered a word, I wasn't sure if he was afraid of Brown or just along for the ride.

An article in Thailand's independent newspaper 'The Nation' certainly reflected Brown's American attitude. It was titled:

> "Ugly American Image Strains US–Asia Ties." Some of the report stated ". . . from Beijing to Bangkok, the image of the United States is taking a beating in Asia. Analysts in the region say it all points to the larger malaise of a superpower using its might to trample on the sensitivities of nations, and in many ways the United States has taken things for granted in Asia, showing little concern of taking into account the complexities of Asian nations cultures, and their peoples."

It was an article that should have been compulsory reading for Brown, as to date his greatest accomplishment in Thailand had been to blacken the eye of his native land.

We left Capt. Chitepong's office and walked the ten minutes to the Royal Orchid Hotel for a coffee. Brown borrowed my mobile and called Dr Pryor describing his conversation with Chitepong, saying he was a ballsy guy and told Pryor, in the presence of Rivers and myself, to either payoff Chitepong and Piboon or have them both shot—a dumb statement to make publicly.

The next day Brown, Dr Pryor and Rivers met with the Thai government Minister Annop. Rivers said several junior members of the US embassy's Commercial Section accompanied them, and that Minister Annop listened to Brown discuss the thirty-inch project and stating he needed an eight month extension to complete and transport the Dredges to Thailand. Minister Annop's response was, 'Go and discuss it with Director General Allrot of the Ports and Rivers Authority, now if you will excuse me, I have other important business to attend to.' Rivers said the minister and his half dozen assistants then left the room, which put Brown right back to square one. He departed Bangkok leaving behind troubled waters.

The following morning, Rivers and myself visited the Prakarn Joint Venture Shipyard and met with Admiral Somboon, the twenty-inch Dredger was nearing completion and would be launched mid February. As I drove Rivers to the airport for his afternoon flight to Baltimore, I discussed my going to New Orleans, he told me no problems; Eastern would take care of all expenses plus a salary increase. He departed, telling me to make arrangements to leave Thailand.

Middle of January, the Inspection Committee visited the Sasco shipyard regarding the construction progress of the Tender Boats. During the visit both Committee Vice Chairman Piboon and Capt. Chitepong informed me the Director General and committee members were extremely upset with Brown because of a three page document he had given to

Minister Annop criticising the Ports and Rivers Authority and their inappropriate actions relating to the thirty-inch project, his refusal to withdraw his derogatory letter, and his lies about the Dredgers being on schedule, when the reports they received from their on-site inspectors confirmed the opposite. Both Piboon and Chitepong asked why no one from the agent Thaitek was present at the Sasco shipyard, as this was an official visit. I told them I had no idea why they weren't present, Piboon said he knew why, they were, 'Thai cowards', and didn't have the courage to face the committee after the lies they had told regarding the under the table commission payments.

CHAPTER 16

Late January, during a telephone call with Rivers I asked about my going to New Orleans, he said the situation had changed, telling me he had been speaking with Brown and the outcome of their conversation was that I could remain employed until the twenty-inch Dredger was complete and then it was termination.

I was perplexed, not expecting to hear this and didn't know whether to laugh or cry. It pissed me off that I would have to find another job, but in a way, I was relieved to be getting out of the Eastern stress and bullshit. Naturally, I asked why the attitude change. Rivers explained that during Brown's ten-day visit to Bangkok, Thaitek's Dr Pryor and Terdsak had continually bombarded him with the statement that I was impeding their performance in dealing with the inspection Committee. The biggest problem was my association with Capt. Chitepong. Brown, thinking as only elitists can think, figured that he and Dr Pryor were ivy-leaguers and therefore Pryor *had* to be trustworthy, and if I was the cause of the problem, then eliminate the problem. Rivers added that Brown, because of his conversations with Pryor, had deduced that I was the 'Bad Egg' so he would rid the project of me and Pryor was to rid the committee of Capt. Chitepong, then all their problems would be solved.

I asked Rivers how Brown figured I could remain until the completion of the twenty-inch project and not consult with the Chairman of the clients' twenty-inch Inspection Committee when that person was Capt. Chitepong. River's response was, he knew it was crazy and sometimes Brown just didn't make sense, but he was the boss. I told Rivers, 'Well fuck it then, it's over, I quit.' After my telephone call with Rivers, I tried to call Brown, but he would not accept my call, his secretary told me he was busy.

The following morning I met Thaitek's Preecha at the Royal Orchid Hotel where we were supposed to go together to the Ports and Rivers Authority building and receive the approved set of fourteen blueprint drawings I had resubmitted several weeks previously. After waiting for an hour, Preecha showed up and dumped the drawings, stamped with the Ports and Rivers Authority's red stamp of approval, on the table where I was sitting in the hotel lounge. 'Here's the drawings, I signed for them, now I have to leave for a meeting.' He stated and was gone. I knew Eastern was hot to receive these drawings, as approval meant savings of thousands of dollars in technical changes for them. I also knew Vice Chairman Piboon was responsible for checking them and ultimately advising the committee to approve them.

Under normal circumstances I would have gone to the hotel's business center and couriered them to Eastern's Baltimore office, but not this time—the more I thought about Brown, the more I wanted to rip his head off and shit down his throat.

Twenty–four hours after being informed of my termination,

Brown telephoned me. I asked him to explain, he responded by saying that after discussions with Thaitek's Dr Pryor, he figured I was upsetting the dynamics of Thaitek's ability to perform, and as he was contractually obligated to continue dealing with Thaitek, it was a business decision. Also, a lot of Eastern money had been invested with Thaitek to secure an extension in construction time, and the decision would stand.

Well I knew Thaitek had received around five million dollars, most of which was for so called under the table commissions, but I also had a contract with Eastern, which Brown disregarded. He told me to return all company property to Thaitek and we would call it quits. After listening to his bullshit rhetoric for several minutes, I told him he was a prick and that for more than a year he had been shitting on me. Well, now it was my turn to shit on him—I had documentation that I would use to cause problems. Cutting in, he asked if I was threatening him, my reply was that I would do what I had to do and angrily slammed the fucken phone down.

I telephoned Capt. Chitepong and we arranged to meet for lunch. During lunch, I explained the situation regarding Eastern and myself. He was surprised and asked, 'Brown did this because you discussed the projects with me?'

'Yes and I can let you listen to both conversations, River's and Brown's, as I have been tape recording our telephone conversations for the past several months as I had a feeling it was all going to turn to shit.'

Through lunch, Capt. Chitepong sympathised with me and the unprofessional manner in which I had been treated. The current movie that was playing in Bangkok was the Mel Gibson classic '*Payback*'. Chitepong asked me if I had seen it and when I confirmed I had, he said to me, 'Well that's what we need—payback!' Before the lunch ended, I told him

Eastern had tricked the inspection committee with regard to the last set of fourteen blueprint drawings they had approved. I explained about the changed technical items they had never received information from Eastern about. He thanked me for the information, saying he would pass it on to Vice Chairman Piboon.

The following day, Thaitek's Preecha telephoned me saying Vice Chairman Piboon wanted the fourteen blueprint drawings returned to the committee. When I asked him why, he said he didn't know, but as he had signed for them could I meet him at the Ports and Rivers Authority building in a couple of hours and he would hand them over? I told him, 'No problem.'

Fifteen minutes later he called me again, requesting I telephone Piboon to advise him that I had already couriered them to Eastern. I asked him why he wanted me to lie to Piboon, he said, 'To help Eastern.' I hung up and did nothing.

Thirty minutes later Preecha called me again and said Piboon had called him and was agitated, and wanted the drawings. Okay, I told him, I would call Piboon, which I did. I told Piboon, 'Regarding the fourteen blueprint drawings, don't worry about them; I will take care of the problem.' I guessed he got the message as he thanked me and hung up.

The following day Preecha called me and asked if I had couriered the drawings to Eastern, I told him no and when he asked why, my response was 'I lost them.' He hung up, ten minutes later, he phoned again asking about the drawings, and again I told him that I lost them. When he asked how, I told him, 'I had set them on the roof of the Isuzu pick-up truck, forgot where I had put them and drove off.'

He became very angry and said, 'This is our last conversation.'

At that point in time I couldn't have given a fat rat's ass, there was only one thing for me to say, so I told him, 'Tell someone who cares!'

Rivers advised me to turn the Isuzu pick-up truck, laptop computer and Eastern documentation over to Thaitek and send an email to Brown requesting two months severance pay. He also asked about the approved set of blueprint drawings, I explained what had happened and how I had supposedly lost them—I had other plans for the drawings. I told Rivers the pick-up truck was legally registered in my name, and therefore there wasn't anything anyone could do about repossessing it. As for the laptop computer, he himself had told me in Baltimore at the beginning of the project I could keep it when the project was over, for me it was over and I was keeping the laptop.

As for the Eastern documentation, well that was a problem he would have to discuss with Eastern's Vice President of Human Resources. Owing to her fucked-up inefficiency, I never signed a company 'Confidentiality Agreement.' Therefore, I intended to hold onto whatever documents I had, and I had many incriminating emails including a copy of the Eastern/Thaitek contract, which, along with the emails, alluded to the misappropriation of $100,000 of the $400,000 training grant from the Trade and Development Agency. It was then that I exposed to Rivers that I had numerous tape recordings of telephone conversations between myself, Brown, the agency Thaitek, inspection committee personnel and himself.

His response was, 'Well I guess you have to do what you have to do, as long as you don't have problems sleeping at night.'

'If I didn't kick some fucken ass and have a little payback on that motherfucker Brown, then I *would* have problems sleeping.'

Over the past year, I had come to understand that Khun

Mechi and all the other Sasco people also wanted payback when it came to Brown.

I knew Khun Mechi had contacted Thaitek's Dr Pryor months earlier and discussed the possibility of joining forces and bringing Brown down. I remembered Rivers had told me that Brown was concerned that if the Trade and Development Agency audited his accounting procedures regarding the $400,000 grant, he could be in trouble.

I was also aware that the United States, for the past twenty years, has had the Foreign Corrupt Practices Act on its statute books barring American firms from paying excess bribes overseas. I had several options. I could turn over the incriminating material, which included full reports on the items manufactured in South Korea that contravened the Eastern/Ports and Rivers Authority contract and the misappropriation of the Trade and Development Agency grant to the United States Embassy's Commercial Department. Or I could approach *The Washington Post* newspaper or Sasco's Khun Mechi, whom I knew had been in the shipping industry in Thailand for the past forty years, with contacts from the organised crime Mafias all the way to the top Thailand government ministers.

I chose Sasco for a beginning, and telephoned their Boat Construction Manager, Bluey and told him of my situation, he told me he would go and speak with MD Chang and call me back. As a precaution I photocopied all documents I thought were harmful to Brown and put them in an envelope and addressed it to the Chairman of the Inspection Committee, I put that envelope inside another envelope, addressed and mailed it to a long-time friend in Canada with a request that should I meet with an unexpected demise, please forward.

CHAPTER 17

BLUEY CALLED ME BACK and asked if I could meet with him and assistant Suwat to discuss my current circumstances. We made an appointment to meet that evening in the 'Cucumber'—a small restaurant tucked away in the Bangna Office complex close to where I was living, that served Thai cuisine. When I arrived, Bluey and assistant Suwat were already seated. After the handshake greetings (neither of which were Masonic) Suwat apologised for MD Chang not being present and added they were not sure of my attitude after having been ordered out of the shipyard by Chang. I told Suwat and Bluey that I fully understood MD Chang's frustration that had caused his outburst as every month I was faced with the same situation, Brown never paid his bills on time, so—Mai Mee Pan Ha.

The question was then asked if I had signed any documentation forbidding me from disclosing any information about Eastern, which I confirmed I had not. Suwat asked if I would consider going to work for Sasco, to which I responded positively.

He then asked if I could give the incriminating Eastern documents I had previously spoken about with Bluey to Sasco. I told him, 'Give me a day or two and you will have them.' We all ate a bowl of khao phad moo (fried rice and pork), drank some Thai Singha beer and made arrangements to meet again in a couple of days, whereupon I would turn over the documents and Sasco would present me with an employment package.

I wasn't looking for employment; all I wanted was payback, so the job offer was a bonus. I had every intention of giving the total documentation package to Khun Mechi and going home to Canada, but what the heck, I was glad to be staying in Thailand, 'The Land of Smiles,' and watch Brown learn that the smiles had teeth!

A couple of days later as previously arranged, I met with Bluey, assistant Suwat and MD Chang at the 'Cucumber'. I presented them with the documents and also the set of fourteen approved blueprint drawings, telling them of the technical changes and that the inspection committee would like them returned. I was given an employment offer, which I accepted and it was decided I would commence work at their shipyard in a couple of weeks.

Chang told me people from Eastern's agent Thaitek had visited his yard on the pretence of bringing a bottle of wine for Chinese New Year, but both Terdsak and Preecha had questioned him and several other Sasco employees, asking if they had been contacted by me. Chang figured that Dr Pryor was worried, and after viewing the documents I had handed over, that Pryor could be in serious trouble with the Thailand tax authorities.

Plus Sasco now had evidence that Thaitek had received monies from Brown to make promised under the table commission payments and had actually lied to government ministers and never paid them. These ministers were friends of Khun Mechi, who could and would, at the appropriate time, expose Thaitek. Chang added that once the information was made public, Thaitek personnel could be in a situation that could ruin their credibility; in fact, they would probably be wise to leave Thailand if they valued their lives. Chang also informed me that Khun Mechi had told him that my name had now been removed from the 'list' of people connected with the Eastern project that were in line to have something adverse done to them!

I visited the Prakarn Joint Venture Shipyard and witnessed the successful launching of the twenty-inch Dredger and spoke with Admiral Somboon and the yard owner Khun Savit. They advised me they would be meeting with the Singaporean representative of the shipping company that had capabilities of transporting the three Dredgers from New Orleans to Bangkok in a couple of days and would I join them. I declined as I was now out of the picture and they would have to deal directly with Rivers.

During the past year, Prakarn shipyard owner, Khun Savit, had been building a small six-inch cutter suction Dredger that would be utilised to keep his launching canal deep enough for the assortment of vessels that came to his yard for repair and also for launching of newly constructed vessels. He also intended leasing it on an hourly basis to other shipyards. It was now completed, launched and was performing dredging trials at his shipyard.

Khun Savit had used my name as the official registered name of the Dredger. I thanked him for the honour and said goodbye to him and Admiral Somboon, they both told me I was welcome to come and visit any time.

The new month rolled around and I went to work for Sasco's shipyard, doing nothing, occasionally assisting Bluey with the construction of the three Tender Boats for the Eastern project. MD Chang had told me that my face was a weapon for Sasco, regarding their struggle for milestone payments from Eastern, he told me Khun Mechi had sent a fax to Brown and Rivers telling them I was now in their employ and he expected Rivers would telephone me to find out what I was doing. He was right, several days later I received a call questioning me about my employment. I told Rivers, seeing as how Eastern had abandoned me without reservation, giving me no return airfare to Canada and no shipping container to transport my household items home as he had promised, I was therefore very fortunate to have received Sasco's offer, which equalled that of Eastern's, and I was still involved with the Eastern Tender Boat project. He sympathised about what had happened saying that was Brown's way, and he was the boss so there was nothing he could do about it. I told him, 'No one can hide from the consequences of the things they do and that includes you and Brown.'

We discussed the situation for several minutes and he told me Brown intended to delay the Sasco milestone keel lay payment. I passed this information on to MD Chang who figured it was about time to send out an anonymous letter to the Ports and Rivers Authority, the Thaitek agency and the Commercial section of the United States embassy, highlighting the corrupt practices of Brown and Thaitek regarding under the table commissions and misappropriation of training funds.

Assistant Suwat returned to me the set of fourteen blueprint drawings I had given to Sasco, saying the vice president of the inspection committee had been inquiring about them. I called Capt. Chitepong and arranged for a Saturday morning meeting to give him the blueprints. I arrived at the Novotel Hotel, Bangna at ten am Saturday morning, and ten minutes later Chitepong, accompanied by the inspection committee Chairman Somwong and Vice Chairman Piboon arrived.

We ordered coffee and I began explaining some of the contractual errors and lies committed by Eastern and Thaitek, Chitepong warned me to be careful of Thaitek people, adding he believed them to be crooks, capable of anything. I asked if he was referring to black unmarked motorcycles, he didn't comment.

Chairman Somwong was extremely disturbed to hear that both Brown and Rivers had lied to him personally and the committee collectively, regarding the manufacturing location of the Dredge pump castings, which was South Korea and not the United States. I handed him the set of Ports and Rivers Authority approved blueprint drawings with the changed technical items. Piboon heaved a sigh of relief. The Chairman thanked me profusely and to my surprise, told me God would bless me for what I had done to assist the committee members—a very Christian statement for a Buddhist. Chitepong told me draftsman Ted had visited Bangkok for several days the previous week and told him that Brown was going to sue me, though on what grounds he didn't know. Well that made two of us.

He added that Ted and Thaitek people had been asking if I had visited with him or any other inspection committee members, both Ted and Thaitek were told that nobody had any idea where I was and there had been no contact.

After a couple of month's involvement at the Sasco shipyard, I got to know several naval architects from the nation of Burma who had worked at the shipyard for years. Both men had been educated in Britain, and told stories of the military dictatorship that ruled their nation and the continued house arrest of the 1991 Nobel Peace Prize Laureate, Aung San Suu Kyi, whom Amnesty International declared a prisoner of conscience and in 1990 had been awarded the 'Sakharn Prize for Freedom of Thought'. The political party Aung San Suu Kyi was affiliated with, the National League for Democracy (NDL) had won the 1989 election by a landslide, securing eighty–two percent of the seats, but the military dictators refused to honour the results. The Burmese guys could not understand why the western nations especially the United States, who preached human rights, had done very little to alleviate the strong-arm tactics of the military junta. These guys were devout Buddhists and heavy into history, they described the current problems of the Hill Tribes that live along the Thai–Burma border, problems that dated back to the turn of the twentieth century when ethnic people fleeing wars and hardships in both Burma and Laos sought asylum in Thailand. Today almost one million of these Hill Tribes people live and farm the rugged lands throughout Thailand's western and northern borders which are remote hilly terrain and largely unmapped. Due to their widespread movements across the Thai–Burma–Laos borders, some Thai authorities accuse these tribal folk of drug production, trafficking and forest destruction. Around fifty percent of Thailand's ethnic Hill Tribe population do not have Thai citizenship and do not have legal rights to the land they farm. These people were born in the Kingdom of Thailand and had lived in the country for generations; nonetheless, they were denied citizenship and birth certificates, all they have been granted is their names. Consequently, their children cannot attend school and no Thai identification cards are issued, a requirement when applying for work—they are Thais that are not Thais.

CHAPTER 18

THE LAST WEEK IN March 1999, the thirty-inch Dredgers should have been delivered but were literally months from completion—by March end; Eastern became liable for $50,000 penalty per day, up to $5 million. Khun Mechi advised MD Chang not to distribute the anonymous letter until all commercial issues were complete. Owing to Eastern not fulfilling its obligation to make milestone payments, Sasco met with Director General Allrot and committee members requesting direct payment, thus bypassing Eastern, Sasco explained, that until payment was received the Tender Boats and Pipelines were their property.

Contractually, Eastern was obligated to supply four million dollars worth of spare parts for the three thirty-inch Dredgers, several million dollars worth had been shipped and were being held in Thai customs. The Ports and Rivers Authority corresponded with Eastern and advised them that payment for the spares would be withheld until an agreement was reached between all parties regarding direct payment to Sasco.

Brown made a one-night stopover visit to Bangkok, signed an amendment to his contract with the Ports and Rivers Authority allowing them to make direct payment to Sasco, he then left town. It gave the impression he was running with his tail between his legs like a mongrel dog.

Late April the Tender Boats were launched, Rivers and Thaitek's Dr Pryor attended the ceremony. Emotionally I wanted to kick ass, but I controlled myself, I shook hands with Rivers and when it was Pryor's turn, he stuck his hand out. For a moment I hesitated, thinking how I wanted to smash my fist into his face, which had lost most of its brown colour and had turned ashen, however it was a controlled macho shake whereby I exerted as much compression as I could. He said nothing— maybe it didn't hurt.

Several days before the launching ceremony, Sasco's owner Khun Mechi had received a fax from Brown and Rivers stating, 'One of your employees have Eastern Dredging Company property, and it must be discussed.' When I questioned Rivers about it, his first reaction was denial of all knowledge of the fax.

'Hey man, I read the Motherfucking fax and saw your fucken signature on the bottom, so quit bullshitting!'

He then admitted that it was in reference to the pick-up truck and laptop computer, I reminded him that ownership papers for the pick-up were in my name because he had offered no assistance for it to be in any other name and he personally had told me I could keep the laptop. He didn't comment further.

Director General Allrot and the inspection committee were also present for the launching and both Piboon and Chitepong told me that the New Orleans shipyard was a disaster, the workforce had been reduced by fifty percent and the schedule was slipping further behind, adding that Brown didn't seem to be disturbed about the fifty thousand dollar per day penalty.

A month after the Tender Boats were launched and the fit-out of the engine rooms, the living quarters and wheelhouse were complete; sea trials were conducted in the presence of the inspection committee. The boats performed better than the required specifications, however there were cosmetic problems the committee wanted adjusted. Several weeks into the repairs, the committee visited Sasco's shipyard for a further inspection, but were still not satisfied, and therefore could not sign off the acceptance certificate.

MD Chang told me he had to make under the table commission payments to all committee members before they would sign off. One of the major complaints by the committee chairman and the ship surveyor was the undersized engine room; they were designed way too small for the amount of installed equipment. Ironically, the committee's vice chairman Piboon was the designer of the vessels and now because of his inadequate design, *he* was receiving illegal payments to accept what *he* in fact had fucked up! Mai Mee Pan Ha—This is Thailand.

Mid July, Sasco received information that Rivers would like to have a meeting and discuss the return of the three thirty-inch Dredgers for construction completion at a shipyard in Thailand. He requested Sasco submit two bid quotes, one for the completion of three Dredgers and one for the completion of two. He told us that Eastern was considering Prakarn, the Joint Venture yard as the location for one Dredge. Several days later, Rivers and Thaitek's Terdsak visited Sasco. I, along with assistant Suwat, met and discussed the remaining work proposal, which was estimated by Eastern to be 78,000 man-hours remaining to complete all three Dredgers.

However, this was just an estimate and being fully aware of

Eastern's history of untruths, I mentioned to Rivers that the suggested man-hours were his and the estimate was based on US shipyards, which had very little relation to Thai shipyards, to which he agreed. The suggested man-hours would need to be tripled to have a more accurate bearing for a Thai yard, as Thai workers are less qualified than their North American counterparts. Thailand does not even have apprenticeship training in the many crafts that are required for shipyard work, mostly it's 'monkey see, monkey do', and many times it's monkey do wrong, meaning rework becomes a costly event in Thailand.

After the meeting, I asked Rivers what the problem was with the New Orleans shipyard. Capt. Chitepong had told me that the yard owner had padlocked the gates, all work had ceased and even the client's inspectors were refused entry. Rivers confirmed the information was correct and the reason was that Brown would not pay $300,000 the shipyard claimed Eastern owed them for rework caused by Eastern's mismanaged engineering department. Seemed the weekend warrior and Ted couldn't get their shit together. Rivers also stated that by returning the Dredgers to Thailand for completion, Brown hoped to renegotiate the penalty clause and not have the five million dollars deducted from his final payout.

The shipyard in New Orleans remained locked down for another three months; meanwhile Director General Allrot had spoken to both Khun Mechi and MD Chang regarding the return of the Dredgers for completion. Before a bid price could be submitted to Eastern, all concerned parties would need to visit the New Orleans shipyard to estimate the remaining work, no one objected to one Dredge being completed at the Joint Venture yard Prakarn, and the remaining two at Sasco. The owner of Prakarn, Khun Savit had informed the Director General that he would travel to view the Dredgers and then submit his price. The Director General suggested that both Sasco and Prakarn should travel to New Orleans together—presenting a united front.

The shipbuilding community in Thailand is extremely competitive and the members are always suspicious of other shipyard intentions, in past years, disagreements had occurred between Sasco and Prakarn. Sasco's reputation was not the most honest in the business. I met with assistant Suwat and MD Chang and discussed the scenario of the returning Dredgers, they asked if I could organise a meeting between both yards to discuss a united front, thus preventing Eastern from playing one yard against the other with the intent of lowering the price.

I contacted Admiral Somboon and informed him of the proposal of unity; he told me he would discuss it with Khun Savit in a day or two and call me. A couple of days later he called and we arranged a dinner meeting. On a Monday evening in late September, Khun Savit, Admiral Somboon, assistant Suwat, MD Chang and myself met at the Thai restaurant called 'The Dairy Queen' in the Bangna suburb of Bangkok.

MD Chang put forward his proposal of a united front, where he would price the scope of work for all three Dredgers, then separate the one costing for Prakarn, if Khun Savit and the good Admiral agreed with all the principals then both shipyards would present a united lump-sum price to Eastern.

This eliminated any potential price manipulation by Brown. All parties agreed this was in their best interest to proceed, also agreeing both shipyard personnel would travel together to New Orleans.

CHAPTER 19

MID OCTOBER, I TRAVELLED with assistant Suwat and Sasco's executive director Khun Mechep, brother of the owner, Khun Mechi to the United States for the Dredger inspection. Khun Savit of Prakarn was ill and would make the journey several weeks later, health permitting.

Rivers met us in New Orleans and drove us to the shipyard where the three thirty-inch Dredgers sat on the bank of the Mississippi river. He told us Brown had departed for Bangkok the previous day to have meetings with his agent, Dr Pryor, and whoever else would give him the time; he was shopping around for another shipyard.

When we arrived at our destination, we were astounded to see parts of the Dredgers all over the shipyard, scattered, rusting; all work had ceased, in reality, the project was a disaster. According to Eastern's on-site consultant, who escorted us on the inspection tour, the shipyard's owner and Eastern's Brown were two peas in a pod—both were belligerent and believed in their own superiority; hence, a breakdown in communication resulted in final arrangements of their contract termination, which was now in the hands of their lawyers.

After the inspection tour, we returned to the Double Tree Hotel on Canal Street, downtown New Orleans, where I had previously stayed with the inspection committee. I sat with Rivers and we discussed the project, Eastern Dredging Co. and the Sasco shipyard. Suwat and Mechep went to sleep off their jet lag. Rivers told me he hoped to float the vessels after they were classified seaworthy by the American Bureau of Shipping hopefully the second week in November; and was negotiating for shipment load-out mid December with the Dredgers arriving in Thailand sometime in February 2000.

As for Eastern, well, several things had occurred since I last had a heart-to-heart discussion with Rivers. Apparently, for more than a year, draftsman Ted and the weekend warrior Johnson had been conspiring to bring about changes within Eastern. One of those changes was the elimination of Eastern's vice president of thirty years. Ted, upholding his backsliding reputation, saw his opening and ratted out Johnson to the vice president in question, which resulted in the termination of Johnson. Ted was rewarded with a promotion to vice president of sales, proof once more, how life is sometimes based on deception.

Rivers continued that he had received his yearly company review by the vice president and Brown, relating that the first several lines praised his efforts and his team attitude, but the remaining two pages accused him of creating most of the problems associated with Eastern's Indonesian and Thailand projects, including the cost overruns.

Rivers added that he had engaged a lawyer and was turning over any documents that may assist him against wrongful dismissal. He also told me his wife was threatening him with divorce. Because of the amount of time he was spending away from her and their three kids whilst attending to the foreign projects, the relationship was deteriorating. He explained how he wanted to see the Thailand project complete and hoped that would have happened by June 2000, as that was the month he had promised his wife he would sever all ties with Eastern.

I decided to tell Rivers that during my initial employment discussions with Sasco MD Chang he had told me that my name had been removed from Khun Mechi's list of people connected to the Eastern project that had to have something nasty done to them, but I had no idea just what that may or may not mean. Rivers then told me that back in February after I had separated from Eastern, he and Thaitek's Dr Pryor were discussing my departure and the information I had accumulated regarding monies Brown had transferred to him regarding illegal under the table commissions that were supposedly made. Pryor was very concerned that I may divulge this information to the Thailand authorities and cause him problems. He told Rivers, 'He had better remember that this is Bangkok.' This could mean only one thing—a black unmarked motorcycle with a passenger riding shooter, and me as the target.

After our return to Thailand from the Inspection tour of the Dredgers, a meeting between the Ports and Rivers Authority and Sasco resulted in Director General Allrot assuring Sasco that they and Prakarn would be the only shipyards to receive approval for the Dredger completion. Sasco had received information, which they turned over to the Director General, indicating that Brown was still contacting each and every shipbuilder in Thailand requesting they forward a bid quote to complete the project.

One shipyard, Oceanthai, threw caution to the wind and bid on the Dredges, an extremely low bid which of course was snapped up by Brown. The Ports and Rivers Authority, as a government department, claimed they could not block Oceanthai and in an astonishing about-face stated that Oceanthai shipyard would be approved. No doubt, Brown had made a sizeable under the table payment, and money does speak all languages.

After several discussions with Sasco's MD Chang regarding the Dredgers and having learned that neither Sasco nor Prakarn had been awarded the contract for completion, there really wasn't any need for my continued employment, so we agreed I would depart. I terminated my employment with Sasco before the supposed arrival date of the Dredges, payback had been my motivation—I wanted to see Brown squirm. I had made arrangements with MD Chang for a sizeable monthly salary loading, which he would have added to his price, this loading would have come out of Eastern's profit, guess some of the Thai fever for graft had rubbed off on me.

I visited one last time with Admiral Somboon whom I considered to be the most honest and un-corruptible person I had dealt with in Thailand, and handed over to him copies of every email, money transfer fax and all other documentation in reference to the Dredger contract, to do with as he pleased.

In the new Millennium, I departed Amazing Thailand, the land of smiles; leaving behind the Rolex Watches, diamond Rings, BMWs and Mercedes-Benz.

CHAPTER 20

I ARRIVED IN CANADA IN the middle of both March and a snowstorm; after the tropical Thai weather—I froze my ass off. I went back to work in the Oil and Gas construction industry but could not let go of the issues that had occurred with the Dredgers and a strong taste for revenge lingered. I read and reread the Eastern Dredger documentation and listened to several hours of the recorded telephone conversations between myself and the Eastern personnel. On one tape, I had Brown admit he had become aware of the $100,000 illegal under the table commission payment from the Trade and Development Agency, therefore I decided to write the agency a letter explaining I had evidence of misappropriation of funds. For a return response address, I rented a post office box and also added a Yahoo email address, shit, how was I to know what information would be passed on to the bad guys? I was trying to lay low but throw shit, hoping it would stick.

Several months later, I received a response thanking me for my letter and an apology for not responding earlier but explained they had, 'taken note of my letter and were currently following the appropriate procedures'.

Another couple of months rolled by and I received an email from a Senior Trial Attorney, Fraud Section, United States Department of Justice, Washington, DC. It stated:

"Your letter to the US Trade and Development Agency concerning improprieties in the contract between Eastern Dredging Co., the Royal Thailand Ports and Rivers Authority and the related Trade and Development Agency training grant, have been forwarded to the Department of Justice for review. We would be interested in evidence that you mention.

We have also been provided with a copy of an article from the Thailand newspaper, The Matichon, from our agent in Bangkok, it also refers to documentary evidence, particularly internal emails from Eastern. If you are in possession of any of the evidence mentioned in the article, or know where it may be located, please forward that information as well.

Once we have had an opportunity to review the evidence, I am sure that we would like to have an opportunity to discuss it with you. Your letter provided only this email address and a post office box; I would appreciate it if you would respond to this email with a telephone number and/ or a street address at which you can be reached. Very Truly Yours . . ."

I let things sit for a while pondering my next move and decided, what the hell, go for it.

I emailed my contact points to the Justice Department and awaited a response remembering that, 'Love and war do not follow the ordinary rules of life', and after all this was my little revenge war.

Several days later, the Department of Justice Attorney called me and asked about the evidence mentioned in their letter and could I forward it to him in Washington DC. He told me after it had been assessed, and if warranted, he would allocate an FBI Agent to the case and arrange a teleconference.

I packaged the documentation and forwarded it, I also included the taped telephone conversation between myself and Brown, where Brown had confirmed his knowledge of the illegal under the table commission of $100,000 paid to Capt. Chitepong. Another couple of weeks went by and utilising the email system, a teleconference was organised between myself, the Department of Justice Attorney and an FBI Agent, who went by the name of Dan.

The conversation was very professional and I was basically asked to explain the whole Dredge scenario including my role as best I could recall. After forty–five minutes of story-telling and questions and answers, Dan the FBI man asked if I would once again contact Eastern Dredging Company and tape the telephone conversation, with questions supplied by himself and the Dept. of Justice, I agreed. But first according to FBI Dan, it would have to be cleared by the Royal Canadian Mounted Police who had federal jurisdiction in Canada, he also asked if I was brought to Baltimore, would I have any hesitation in meeting with some of the Eastern Dredge Company players and wear a wire, I told him I had no qualms.

Ten days later FBI Dan called me and advised that the RCMP had vetoed the taping of telephone conversations, apparently in Canada it is only legal to tape telephone conversations in relation to the illicit narcotic trade. He then said if I was agreeable, he would make flight arrangements for me to come to Baltimore and meet with himself and the Dept. of Justice, I agreed.

Recalling an old saying, 'keep your friends close and your enemies closer', I decided to give Rivers a call at Eastern. During the conversation I told him the Dept. of Justice had been in contact with me about the Dredger deal in Thailand, his response was that Brown was in litigation with the Ports and Rivers Authority, the shipyard Oceanthai had upped their price to complete the Dredgers and everything was in total disarray regarding the Dredger contract. He also told me that Terdsak from the Thaitek agency had stated Capt. Chitepong was ready to put a contract out on me for spilling the beans on the corruption. This caught me by surprise, I had sent a letter to Admiral Somboon and informed him I had been in contact with the Dept. of Justice but I didn't believe he would have told Capt. Chitepong.

I decided to telephone Chitepong and ask him what shit he was up too. He was very friendly until I laid the Terdsak statement on him about giving me a bunch of pain, he responded by saying if someone hurt him he must hurt them back. I wanted to know what the fuck that meant. His response was that the Matichon newspaper had printed several articles regarding the corrupt practices at the Ports and Rivers Authority and the evidence they reported consisted of Eastern emails and faxes dealing with the Dredger contract and he figured it must have been me who handed over the information. I then told him about the email I had received from the Matichon newspaper requesting any evidence I might have which would enhance the emails and faxes already in their possession, this information surprised him and he seemed to be at loss for words. I added I'd send him a copy of the email and he could check out the date it was sent and the date the articles were printed and he would see I had received the email after the newspaper reports, which meant they had received their information before they had contacted me.

I reminded him of another fact, which was that I had turned over copies of all the Eastern documentation to the Sasco shipyard as a condition of my employment agreement.

Before he accused me of wrongdoing he needed to look in his own back yard, and while he was at it, find out who the fuck had given the Matichon newspaper my email address. He said he would, changing the subject by asking about my new job in Canada and ending the conversation by wishing me well. That was my last conversation with Capt. Chitepong; however, I did forward the Matichon email for his information.

Within a couple of days of my conversation with Rivers, I received a telephone call from a lawyer in Chicago acting on behalf of the Eastern Dredging Company. I listened to this guy, who for fifteen minutes never let up about Brown, Eastern Dredging, its history, Thai corruption, himself, and how he used to work for then Mayor of New York, Mayor Giuliani. He finished up by offering on behalf of Brown and the Eastern Co., a lawyer to represent me, at no cost, for any future dealings with the FBI or the Dept. of Justice. I told him I would think about it.

After my return to Canada, I hooked up with the internet and would go onto the 'Bangkok Post' newspaper web page and from time to time, there would be articles referring to the wrong doings at the Ports and Rivers Authority. Shit was beginning to happen, the Thai National Counter-Corruption Commission was now in the picture and they were investigating the corrupt practices between the Authority and Eastern. The newly elected Prime Minister went on national television and stated he would rid Thailand of the existing corrupt dealings of government departments and in particular, he would make an example of the Ports and Rivers Authority, as they had cost the Thai government $50 million (1.95 billion Baht).

Chapter 21

SIX WEEKS BEFORE SEPT 11 2001, FBI Dan couriered the round-trip airline tickets to me. During his telephone call to check if I had received them, he told me he would meet me at the luggage collection carousel at the Baltimore Washington International airport, he also asked for a description of myself so that he would be able to recognise me. I told him I was five foot nine, bald with a large beer-belly; in actuality I was over six foot with a full head of greying hair and a medium beer-belly. Shit by this time I was a little paranoid, I had no idea what or whom may be waiting for me in Baltimore, I had no idea of who was in cahoots with whom, for all I knew, some ass bag hit-man might be waiting for me.

I arrived at BWI airport around five pm, collected my luggage and began to search the crowd that had gathered to pick up arriving passengers. I purposely walked by a dark suit, the wearer looked directly at me then looked away searching the crowd. I stood several yards from this guy and made like I was waiting for a lift, he continuously searched the faces of the coming and going, he was the only dark suit,

I figured Hollywood had got it right. I waited another couple of minutes, then walked up to him and asked his name, he responded, Dan, I introduced myself, he looked at me and said, you didn't give a true description of yourself, no, I said, that was my stealth. He produced his FBI identity as he led the way to his blue Chevy Impala.

During the journey to the Sunshine Inn, FBI Dan informed me that the Trade and Development Agency illegal payment of $100,000 would probably be the most damaging evidence against Eastern's owner, Brown. He continued, saying how he would be interested to hear the other tape recordings of telephone calls and would have them transcribed, I confirmed I had them with me. We arrived at the Inn and FBI Dan led the way to the suite he had previously booked for me, telling me he had checked me in under an assumed name, man this was Hollywood cloak-and-dagger shit in reality. He handed me the key card as I handed him the stack of eight mini cassette tapes. Dan told me he would return at nine the following morning with the Department of Justice Senior Trial Attorney from the Fraud Section, he would be the same guy I had spoken with on the telephone. FBI Dan also advised me that should I have any problems with anyone or anything, to immediately call him on his cell phone or pager, other than that he would see me in the morning.

Nine am next morning, both parties arrived. FBI Dan removed his revolver from its holster, put on a trigger lock and placed it on the closet shelf where he hung his jacket and told me the cassette tapes were being transcribed.

The Department of Justice Attorney, Dan and myself sat in the living room of the hotel suite and discussed the shit that went down in Thailand, bribes that were paid, Thaitek's manipulation of all concerned and the role I had played. During the conversation, the Department of Justice Lawyer stated that he had been contacted by the Matichon newspaper out of Bangkok and asked if they had contacted me. I admitted they had sent me an email asking for any evidence I might have, I also told him that before I had left Bangkok one of their investigative reporters had phoned me and asked me to assist them with their investigation of the Dredger contract. I had told the reporter if I did as he requested I would be found floating in the Chao Praya river, the reporter responded by saying my identity would never be revealed, in fact I could be the newspaper's 'Deep Throat' in reference to the past US President Nixon's Watergate scandal, I had told them no. I also added that before I left Thailand, I had contacted the Commercial Attaché at the United States embassy in Bangkok, the Embassy people informing me they were very much aware of the activities of Eastern Dredging Company and its owner Brown.

After I told them what I knew about the under the table pay off's and the documentation I possessed, their advice was, 'We won't tell you to deliver the evidence to us, and we won't tell you *not* to deliver the evidence to us. However if you do deliver it to us, we will, under US law, be obliged to follow up with an investigation, so the decision is yours.' It was then that I told the Attorney and FBI Dan about the lawyer who had called me on behalf of Brown and his company Eastern, who offered me representation free of charge. The attorney asked for the lawyer's name and offered to shut him down immediately if I wanted, I told him, 'Go ahead.' I never heard from the lawyer again.

Around ten–thirty the first morning, we were visited by another FBI Agent who had bought the Per Diem payment for me. FBI Dan had me sign a receipt covering four days at $210 per day, which included the two days of travel, utilis-ing the codename: 'Dredge'. I signed 'Dredge', but felt like a dickhead doing it. The remainder of the day was spent going through the Eastern documents, faxes, emails and contracts with the Department of Justice attorney and FBI Dan, both asking questions until they got the shit strait in their heads.

The following day only FBI Dan showed up and we walked through the taped telephone conversations. Until I had listened to most of the tapes, I hadn't realised how much I had cussed during the conversations—by the end of six or seven hours of listening, to my amusement old Dan the FBI man was cussing up a storm, I guessed all that swearing he'd been listening to had penetrated his brain. The following morning, Dan picked me up at the Sunshine Inn and drove me to the Baltimore Washington International airport for my eight am flight back to Canada.

My contact with both the Department of Justice and FBI had surprised me, perhaps by their professional behaviour, but then again I had not been sure just what to expect, all in all, it had felt like beautiful payback.

Over the ensuing months, I had several conversations with FBI Dan, discussing several articles that had been printed in the 'Bangkok Post', which I had read on their Web page. The articles told about the ongoing investigation of the Ports and Rivers Authority and the Dredger scandal. I learned from FBI Dan that Brown's wife had divorced him, citing his business practices as too stressful for their relationship. Brown's father, who had bought him Eastern Dredging Company, had died of old age, and the American Export Import bank had foreclosed on their loans to Eastern and repossessed the company, eventually selling it to an Egyptian Dredging outfit. Dan also told me Brown and his lawyers were negotiating with the Department of Justice lawyers and he would possibly receive a fine, but it did not appear that there would be a Grand Jury investigation. Oh well, I figured, what the hell, at least I had the monkey off my back and it felt good.

The new owners of Eastern had fired a bunch of former Eastern employees, including draftsman Ted and Rivers; also things were happening in Thailand. I read on the 'Bangkok Post' web page that charges would be laid in the very near future against senior members of the Ports and Rivers Authority in relation to the contract for the Dredgers to be built by the Eastern Dredging Company of Baltimore, Maryland, USA. The Thai government had cancelled the contract with Eastern and the new owners, believing to continue with the deal would be throwing more good money after bad— trying to recover the three Dredgers and shipping them to Thailand for construction completion. The article also stated that as the contract was cancelled, the Export Import bank in Baltimore had sold the uncompleted Dredgers to another Louisiana shipyard.

After reading the article, I telephone FBI Dan and asked him if he was aware of the situation in Thailand, he responded the FBI had submitted all the evidence I had supplied him including the taped telephone conversations to their FBI Agent stationed at the American Embassy in Bangkok. He in turn had submitted all evidence to his counterpart within the Thailand Justice system. After hearing that, I figured I had better take Thailand off any future travel itinerary.

Several months later, I was cruising the 'Bangkok Post' web site when the headline jumped right at me,

"Seven Charged in Dredger Deal Scandal, Case goes to court, suspects out on bail."

"Seven Ports and Rivers Authority officials including the Director General, were charged with abuse of authority in connection with the Dredger procurement scandal. The indictment came

*after the Thai National Counter-Corruption Commission
found the seven officials guilty of wrongdoing, which caused
damages worth more than one billion Baht to the state. The
defendants wrongfully endorsed the handover of parts of the
Dredgers, allowing the contractor to claim payment of up to
85 percent of the project cost, despite being unable to complete
construction on time. The Criminal Court accepted the lawsuit,
releasing the defendants on 500,000-Baht bail each. All
denied the charges.*

*The contract was signed with Eastern Dredging Company
in September 1997 for three Dredgers. The $50 million con-
tract originally required Eastern to complete the Dredgers by
March 1999; the Thai Government extended the deadline to
February 2001. However, the Ports and Rivers Authority had
never seen the Dredgers, which were 34 percent complete, while
85 percent of the project cost had been paid to Eastern. The
contract was scrapped by the newly-elected Thai government
and about a month later, the US firm went bankrupt."*

After reading the article, I was stunned and surprised,
knowing there was a rich man's law and a poor man's law
in the strongest sense in Thailand. I never thought charges
would be laid against these guys, I always figured they would
have paid off any official that could cause them harm. I was
also curious as to why there was no mention of Eastern's agent
Thaitek, I guessed in their case they must have spread some
cash around, but then they had gathered up over five million
dollars from the Dredger deal and I guessed they had kept the
lion's share of that. I knew they had very powerful political
connections, connections bought and paid for. I continued to
read the 'Bangkok Post' web site, curious to learn the outcome
of my old cohorts at the Ports and Rivers Authority.

I didn't have long to wait—two months after they had

been released on bail, the shit hit the Thai fan big time—not only was the Thai National Counter Corruption Commission investigating the Ports and Rivers Authority officials but so was the Anti-Money-Laundering Office of the Thai government.

Director General Allrot and six of his Inspection Committee members, including my old pal Capt. Chitepong and his close associate Inspection Committee Vice Chairman Piboon were found guilty by the Anti-graft Agency of abuse of authority, corruption and causing damages worth more than one Billion Baht to the State.

A surprise raid on Director General Allrot's place of residence, uncovered 10 million Baht in 1,000 Baht bills stashed in a closet. Allrot could not satisfactorily explain how he had come by the cash, leading to the impounding of his assets, which included five houses in various up-market suburbs of Bangkok, six luxury motor vehicles (including the latest models of BMW, Mercedes-Benz and Lexus) plus a cache of a half dozen men's Rolex watches—each with a retail value of more than $10,000 a piece.

Assets belonging to the Inspection committee members were also impounded, as the authorities learned they had utilised their relatives to launder the ill-gotten loot from the Dredger procurement scandal for numerous investments in high fashionable houses, Rolex watches, $800 a-piece Mont Blanc fountain pens and luxury automobiles.

This I knew was a huge 'loss of face' for these guys, which is an extremely serious cultural affliction in most all South East Asian nations. I believed this would not be the end of the Dredger saga; somehow, someday, someone had to pay. I just hoped it wouldn't be me, after all, the only thing I really got out of the Dredger contract was the shitty end of the stick.

A couple of months rolled by when another startling turn

of events came across the internet web site with the headlines, *"DREDGER SCANDAL – Arrest warrant issued"*. I was astounded at how the Thai authorities were pursuing the Dredge catastrophe, I guessed the current Prime Minister hadn't exaggerated when he stated on national television shortly after taking office, that he was going to '. . . eliminate corruption from his government departments and intended to make an example of the Ports and Rivers Authority officials'.

The arrest warrant was issued for the apprehension of Dr. Pryor, senior partner of the Thaitek Agency, which had acted as the third party representative between Eastern Dredging Company of Baltimore USA, and the Ports and Rivers Authority for the Cutter Suction Dredger project.

The warrant stated that Dr Prior was involved in misappropriation of government funds and laundering Dredger Project payments through his Singapore bank account and evading his taxation obligations in Thailand.

However, the elusive Dr Prior was nowhere to be found in Thailand and it was suspected he might have absconded to Europe, possibly Switzerland.

Obviously, I had been wrong about the payoffs I thought Prior would have made to save his hide, but on the other hand he did have a big ass-national and just maybe his political connections thought he was too hot a potato to handle.

After reading about these developments I remembered what Sasco's MD Chang had mentioned to me in the 'Cucumber' restaurant, and that was, if the information was made public regarding illegal under the table payments, Thaitek's Dr Prior could be in a situation that could ruin his credibility. In fact, Chang had said Prior would probably be wise to leave Thailand if he valued his life. Well, the cat was out of the bag and I believed without a doubt if Dr Prior returned to Thailand he wouldn't have long to wait before a black unmarked motorcycle drew up alongside his vehicle with a well-trained shooter riding passenger.

I was now mentally back in the Bangkok saddle with enthusiasm, each day opening up the '*Bangkok Post*' web page, eagerly awaiting new developments, and I wasn't to be disappointed. Several months after the warrant for Dr Prior was issued, judgment was handed down from the Thai court sentencing the Ports and Rivers lawbreakers to terms in the 'Monkey House' of five years for Director General Allrot, three years each for Capt. Chitepong and committee Vice Chairman Piboon, with the remaining four committee members each receiving two years. The impounded assets of all convicted felons would remain property of the state.

Lawyers for the Ports and Rivers offenders stated they would be appealing the sentences.

I was finding it hard not think about Capt. Chitepong; basically he was a good guy, certainly a greedy guy, but with a great sense of humour and doing time in the 'Monkey House' would not go down well for him and the 'loss of face' would be devastating. Oh well, I guessed it wasn't worth me worrying about the shit I had no control over, as the saying goes, 'If you can't do the time, don't do the crime'.

Six or seven months went by, I continued to casually read the '*Bangkok Post*' web page to basically stay in touch with that part of the world, I had mostly forgotten about the Dredgers and the shit that went with them, when out of the blue, wham, there it was. The headline was electrifying; I got goose bumps as I read it.

"American Assassinated in Taxi.

According to the police report, a taxi driver picked up his passenger from the Royal Orchid Hotel in downtown Bangkok situated on the banks of the Chao Praya River around three in the morning and was instructed by the hotel's bellhop to drive the guest to Bangkok's Don Muang International airport.

After several minutes of travelling on the almost deserted four-lane Don Muang toll-way the taxi driver noticed a car pursuing his cab. As the mysterious car got closer to the rear of his taxi, the driver decided to speed up in order to keep a safe distance, however the pursuing vehicle finally overtook the taxi and immediately cut in front causing a minor collision before both vehicles came to a standstill.

The taxi driver got out of his cab hoping to negotiate with the driver of the other vehicle regarding repair costs; he stopped cold in his tracks when he saw a man getting out of the other vehicle with a pistol in each hand running towards him. Before the taxi driver could react, the pistol-packing gunman reached the cab and, utilising both pistols, shot to death the passenger who was seated in the rear of the taxi. Following the shooting, the gunman glanced at the taxi driver as he walked back to his waiting vehicle and was driven away by his accomplice. The assassinated American was identified as Edward Brown, former president and owner of the now-bankrupt Eastern Dredging Company of Baltimore, Maryland, USA, the company that had forfeited on a contract to build three Dredges for the Royal Thailand Ports and Rivers Authority."

THE END

LONG IS THE NIGHT TO HIM WHO IS AWAKE

LONG IS A MILE TO HIM WHO IS TIRED

LONG IS A LIFE TO THE FOOLISH

WHO DO NOT KNOW THE TRUE LAW

Dhammapada.

ALSO BY TONY MAY
AVAILABLE FROM SID HARTA PUBLISHING

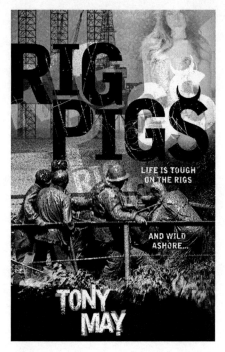

Life on the oil rigs is tough. Aside from the constant danger of explosions, accidents and sub-standard safety procedures, there are the other workers to contend with. You meet a lot of weird characters out there on the rigs; all are memorable, and many have a heart of gold underneath their mean exteriors. 'Rig Pigs', the rough and tumble men who work the oilfields in the middle of the ocean, are often as dangerous and difficult as the work they do. But man, do they know how to raise hell! When they are let loose in cities all over the world when their rig time is done, it's the booze, women and bars that keep them going until their next 'tour of duty'.

But in the seventies, there is another tour of duty for many, and it's taking place in Vietnam. While one man travels the world, partying with his oil rig cohorts and living the high life, he is thinking of his brother, Terry, fighting the war in Vietnam. One day he receives the news that will change their lives, and their relationship – Terry is coming home to face an even bigger battle ... and he needs his brother by his side.

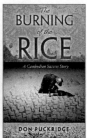
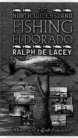

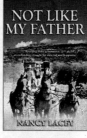

Best-selling titles by Kerry B. Collison

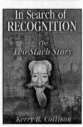

Readers are invited to visit our publishing websites at:
http://www.sidharta.com.au
http://www.publisher-guidelines.com/
http://temple-house.com/

Kerry B. Collison's home pages:
http://www.authorsden.com/visit/author.asp?AuthorID=2239
http://www.expat.or.id/sponsors/collison.html
http://clubs.yahoo.com/clubs/asianintelligencesresources
email: author@sidharta.com.au

Purchase Sid Harta titles online at
http://www.sidharta.com.au